ROCK

SHADOWRIDGE GUARDIANS MC

BECCA JAMESON

PHOTOGRAPHY BY
ASHLEY CONVERSE PHOTOGRAPHY

COVER MODEL
KEVIN DAVIS

ABOUT SHADOWRIDGE GUARDIANS MC

Combining the sizzling talents of bestselling authors **Pepper North, Kate Oliver, and Becca Jameson,** the Shadowridge Guardians are guaranteed to give you a thrill and leave you dreaming of your own throbbing motorcycle joyride.

Are you daring enough to ride with a club of rough, growly, commanding men? The protective Daddies of the Shadowridge Guardians Motorcycle Club will stop at nothing to ensure the safety and protection of everything that belongs to them: their Littles, their club, and their town. Throw in some sassy, naughty, mischievous women who won't hesitate to serve their fair share of attitude even in the face of looming danger, and this brand new MC Romance series is ready to ignite!

Shadowridge Guardians MC
Steele by Pepper North
Kade by Kate Oliver
Atlas by Becca Jameson
Doc by Kate Oliver
Gabriel by Becca Jameson

Rock

"Baby girl, if you think I'll let you walk out that door when I just got you back, you are sadly mistaken."

Lyla left her hometown almost forty years ago and never looked back. It's time to return to Shadowridge, clean out her parents' rental, and put it up for sale. But coming home brings back memories of her first love, the man who rocked her world for one night—a man she never saw again after that summer.

Rock has been with the Shadowridge Guardians for his entire adult life. His first love left town, taking his heart with her. He lost his second love, his wife, to cancer several years ago. Rock considers himself too old to risk love a third time, but then he learns Lyla is back in town…

After four decades, he can't stop thinking of her. He needs to know why she left. He needs to look her in the eyes. But what if confronting her doesn't purge her from his system?

ROCK: THE PREQUEL

The following short story was originally publishing in the 2023 Dirty Daddies Anniversary Anthology. It is a prequel to *Rock*, and I'm republishing it again here. If you've already read *Rock: The Prequel*, you can skip to the full book, *Rock*, in the table of contents. Or, maybe you want to read *The Prequel* again!

PROLOGUE

F*orty years ago…*

"Get out, punk."

Lyla lifted her face to glare in the direction her brother would soon make his appearance. He hadn't even fully descended the stairs and rounded the corner before he was already demanding she leave the basement. Why he thought he owned the basement she would never understand, but every time he had friends over, he kicked her out and made her go upstairs. As if she wanted to hang with their parents any more than he did.

She could hear two sets of footsteps pounding down the wooden stairs, which meant he only had one friend with him this afternoon. Hopefully it wasn't Mark or Jeff. Both of them were douchebags. The others were usually friendly or indifferent toward her.

Gaze narrowed, she caught his eyes as soon as he came into view. "I'm in the middle of something."

"Don't care. Do it upstairs in your room," Jackson demanded.

A second later, his friend stepped into her line of sight, and Lyla's breath hitched. This wasn't Mark or Jeff or any other friend she'd ever met. This guy was new. He was also hot.

Lyla set her pencil down on the table and quickly closed her sketchbook. She didn't like anyone seeing her drawings. Ever. She returned her gaze to the newcomer. It was hard to look away.

He was tall. Six foot. Broad. His brown hair was in need of a cut. He hadn't shaved for a few days. Or perhaps he simply hadn't shaved today. The guy had on a worn black leather jacket with some kind of patch, and when he took it off seconds later and draped it over his arm, her breath hitched again.

His arms were huge, much bigger than any other boy she knew at school. And he had a tattoo.

Lyla's mouth went completely dry. She had no idea why she was so attracted to this guy. Her parents would shit if she ever dated someone like him, and that thought alone almost made her giggle.

At sixteen, she'd only been permitted to date for the past month, and so far, it hadn't happened anyway. It was kind of a moot issue. Lyla wasn't exactly a member of the "in" crowd. She had stringy brown hair, glasses, and braces. Boys weren't lined up, waiting for her to turn sixteen, so she could go on dates.

Jackson snatched an apple from the basket across from her, the fruit basket she'd been sketching for art class. He took a bite, the crunch sounding loud in the silence.

She jerked her attention back to him. "Hey, I was using that."

He shrugged. "You know Mom and Dad are never going to let you go to art school. I don't know why you bother sitting around drawing shit." He took another bite.

She flinched. She was well aware her parents thought she should become a teacher or a nurse. That didn't mean she intended to ignore her passion. She could always sketch as a hobby.

Jackson nodded toward the stairs. "Rock and I have homework to do. Beat it."

Her eyes widened as she shifted her attention back to the tattooed hunk. *Rock.* Even his name was sexy. "Homework..." she deadpanned.

Rock smirked. "Calculus."

"So, you're here to help my brother." She gathered her own books and her sketch pad. She'd already finished all her homework earlier, and she knew her brother well enough to surmise he'd asked this new guy over to help him. Math wasn't his strongest subject.

Rock's brows went up as he stared at her. Finally, he shrugged. "We're just going to study together."

Interesting. The guy didn't want to throw her brother under the bus.

Jackson finished his apple and tossed the core into the trashcan. "You can leave now."

Lyla shot him another glare. "Don't get your panties in a wad. I'm going. And I won't tell anyone you have a math tutor either." After stepping around the table, she hugged her books to her chest and headed for the stairs.

Maybe she walked a bit closer to Rock than absolutely necessary. Maybe she inhaled deeply as she approached him. Maybe she would never forget his scent as it filled her nose. He was no boy. He was a man. He was undoubtedly a senior like her brother and probably eighteen, but he gave off a vibe of someone older. Wiser. More solid.

"Shit. Forgot drinks and snacks. I'll be right back," Jackson declared before he bounded back up the stairs.

"Sorry," Rock murmured.

She paused next to him. "For what?"

"Didn't mean to kick you out. You were here first."

She smiled, even though she knew she was nowhere close to being in his league, what with her mouthful of braces and total lack of makeup. She pushed her glasses up on her nose. "It's okay. I'm used to it. Jackson's a good guy. He just likes to posture in front of his friends."

"Mmm. Not sure I like how he speaks to you."

A shiver wracked her body. Was this guy sticking up for her? She squeezed her books tighter against her small breasts, grateful the cover was keeping him from noticing how young she was or that her nipples were suddenly hard.

His voice. *Yikes.* Deep and sensual. He never looked away.

She licked her dry lips, unable to keep moving past him.

"You're in calculus too, aren't you?" Rock asked. "I think I've seen you coming out of the third-period class."

Stunned didn't begin to describe how she felt. She gaped at him. "Yes," she whispered. "I could help my brother myself, but he doesn't like it when I do. Emasculating or something."

Rock chuckled, the deep resonating sound making her heart race. "I understand that."

She lowered her gaze to the jacket draped over his arm to avoid the intensity of everything that was Rock. When her eyes landed on the sleeve, she leaned in closer. "Is that patch a teddy bear with wings?"

He held it up for her to see better. "Yep. I'm a member of the Shadowridge Guardians MC. It's our logo."

"A motorcycle club?" She felt stupid for asking. Duh. Obviously.

"Yep."

She'd never known anyone from a motorcycle club, but she knew one existed in town. "Aren't you kind of young to belong to an MC?" she asked before she could filter herself. *Shut up, Lyla. Just. Shut. Up.*

He didn't seem upset by her question. He simply shrugged. "My parents are members."

Ah. So he's like a legacy or something.

He nodded toward the fruit bowl. "You're an artist."

She shook her head. "No. I just dabble. It's nothing really."

"Can I see?"

Eyes wide again, she gaped at him. "Not a chance."

His lips rose in a slow smile before he reached up and tucked a lock of hair behind her ear. His rough fingers lingered. "Okay. Keep your secrets. But I'm going to ask again, and one day you're going to show me what you're hiding, Little Lyla."

She sucked in a breath. Every inch of her body was on fire. The hottest boy/man she'd ever seen was standing inches away from her. He was still toying with her earlobe, and he was looking her right in the eye.

She glanced at his full lips, her overactive imagination wishing he would kiss her. That was absurd of course. He surely had women fawning all over him. Not girls. Women. Sexy women with nice boobs and skimpy skirts. Women with fancy hair, makeup, contacts, and perfect teeth.

"I should go upstairs," she murmured.

"Yeah, you probably should." His half smile caused her tummy to flutter. "Think of me when you're sketching. Remember: One day I'm going to look through that sketchpad, Little Lyla."

Why did he call her that? She couldn't make sense of it, but it did something to her. It made a knot form in her stomach. She didn't want to go upstairs. She wanted to stay down here with this man who was giving her his undivided attention. She wanted him to look at her like that for hours, stroke her hair, speak to her in that sexy, rough voice, and call her Little Lyla.

In your dreams.

The sound of her brother stomping back down the stairs made her flinch and take a giant step back. Her face flushed as if she'd done something naughty and was about to get caught.

She'd done a lot of naughty things, in her head at least. All sorts of naughty ideas flitted through her mind. She'd never kissed a boy before, but she'd bet this man could kiss like a real man. She'd bet he could do other things too, and she'd love to experience them.

Don't be ridiculous.

"Why are you still down here?" Jackson demanded as he jumped the last few steps to the basement floor.

"I'm going. I'm going." She could feel Rock's heavy stare on her. It never wavered as her brother rushed past them, his arms laden with cans of soft drinks and bags of chips.

As she turned toward the stairs, forcing herself not to look back at Rock one last time, he grabbed her hand and leaned in to whisper in her ear. "Tell me you'll never stop sketching. Never stop following your heart."

"Okay." She bit her lower lip, frozen as his breath teased her ear.

"Good girl."

CHAPTER
ONE

Two years later…

"Shit," Lyla muttered under her breath as she parked her car in the driveway. She turned off the engine and stared out the passenger window at the Harley parked in the street in front of her house.

Normally, the sight of that Harley made her pulse race, her hands become clammy, and her panties dampen. But not tonight. Tonight she just wanted to be alone. She wanted to slink into the house, tiptoe up the stairs, lock her bedroom door, flop onto her bed, and wallow in self-pity.

She glanced at the dash clock. It was after eleven. The house was dark except for the small lamp in the front window her mother always left on at night. Thank God her parents were already in bed.

Now she had to get past Rock. And unfortunately, her brother. She wasn't in the mood for twenty questions. She needed a bath and a good cry so she could lick her wounds.

It didn't surprise her that Rock was here. He was here a lot. She'd never understood the relationship he had with her brother. It seemed to her like the two of them were polar opposites. But they'd remained friends, even though her brother had just finished his sophomore year in college.

Rock had gone to school too. He'd gone to the local community college. She knew he'd gotten his associates in business and was about to do an internship somewhere this summer.

Taking a deep breath, Lyla finally opened the door of her coupe and carefully climbed out. She smoothed down the front of her tight black skirt and headed for the side door next to the garage. *Maybe I can sneak in undetected and slink up the stairs.*

The kitchen was quiet and dark. She shut the door as gently as possible, facing it as she turned the lock. The house was eerily silent. Instead of the usual music and laughter or television she expected to hear coming from the basement, she heard nothing.

"How was the prom, Little Lyla?"

The sound of Rock's deep voice coming from right behind her made her nearly jump out of her skin. She spun around so fast, she almost tripped on her three-inch heels. "You scared me." She flattened her hand on her chest.

Rock's eyes widened as he took a step back. His gaze roamed up and down her body several times, blatantly checking her out. "Shit…" he breathed out.

She trembled as she watched him in the long beam of moonlight coming through the kitchen window.

They stood that way for long seconds, him fucking her with his gaze, her nearly melting. It was a wonder her knees held up. She'd had the hots for him for two years. He'd teased and flirted with her off and on, but he'd never looked at her the way he was looking at her now.

"Come." He reached forward and took her hand. "I want to hear all about it, starting with why you're home so early and why you're alone. I know you went to the prom with that Brinkman kid, Casper or Jasper or whatever his name is."

Rock instantly chased away some of her sorrow with his silly comment, and she almost laughed as he dragged her toward the basement stairs. Then reality seeped in.

She tugged her hand to break the connection and backed up to flatten herself once again to the back door. She was breathing heavily as she shook her head. The last thing she needed or wanted was to sit down and talk to Rock right now. She was nursing wounds. He would suck the air out of the basement with his scent and his smile and his touch.

Rock had no idea she secretly harbored a crush on him unlike any other crush ever held by a girl in all of time. He had no idea the shit night she'd had or that she'd been on the verge of tears when she entered the house. He had no idea his kindness would cause her to slide into the ugliest ugly cry on earth, which would make her feel even worse when she woke up tomorrow, having let him see her vulnerable side.

No way was she going to the basement with Rock Monroe.

Rock turned back toward her and stepped closer. "What's wrong?"

"Where's Jackson?" she asked, ignoring his question.

Rock rolled his eyes. "Drank too much. Passed out in his room."

"Why are you here?"

"I waited for you." His voice was so damn kind. Why was he always so kind to her?

"Why?"

He reached up and lifted one of the perfect curls still hanging from her updo, a ringlet that hadn't dared to collapse since it had enough hairspray on it to shellac the planet. His voice was soft when he met her gaze. "I couldn't leave until I knew you were home safe, and I want to hear about the prom."

She held his gaze. They did this often. Stared at each other without speaking. She usually fled to her room after such an instance, threw herself on her bed, and stared at the ceiling, pretending the two of them were long-suffering forbidden lovers or some other sappy shit from romance novels.

She licked the seam of her lips, wondering if her bold red lipstick was still in place. "I can't, Rock. Not tonight. I'm exhausted and…" *Shit. Shit shit shit.* A tear escaped.

She lifted a hand to dash it away and turned her head to one side.

"Fuck," he muttered before closing the distance even more. He cupped the side of her face. "I need you to talk to me, Baby girl."

Another tear fell, and another. She shook her head.

"Come with me," he encouraged.

She looked toward the stairs.

"Not to the basement. Come to my apartment. You need someone to talk to. I want to be that man, Little Lyla. We'll go on my bike. If your parents look outside, they'll see your car and assume you got home safely."

She didn't even blink as she held his gaze again. "You're serious."

"Totally. We can walk to the next block and I'll start up the bike there so it won't wake up anyone in the house. I'll bring you back in a few hours. Come with me."

She bit her bottom lip. She'd had a crush on Rock for two years. The king of all crushes. This was a horrible plan. There was no way he saw her as more than his friend's kid sister. Which she was.

In a few days, he was going to leave town for his internship. At the end of the summer, she would go away to college.

She might never have an opportunity like this again. A chance to be alone with Rock Monroe—sexiest man she'd ever seen. It didn't matter if this was the only night she ever got with him. At least she would have spent a few hours with him alone. That time could provide fodder for her daydreams for months or years.

It could also destroy her.

She hedged.

"Don't think. Come." He grabbed her hand again. "Say yes."

She swallowed. She knew this was a bad idea, but she couldn't say no to him. Ever. "Okay."

CHAPTER
TWO

"Sorry. I didn't think about your dress," Rock said five minutes later as soon as he'd led her around the corner to the next street.

Damn, she was smoking hot. This was probably the worst idea in the history of all ideas. What had he been thinking, insisting she go to his apartment with him?

He wasn't about to stop now, though. She was here. Right next to him. Glancing around adorably, as if she was worried someone might see them.

And that dress. *Fuck. Me.* It should have been illegal. All black and silky and hugging her curves like it was made for her. Hell, considering who her parents were, maybe it had been made for her. Her family certainly had money.

The material clung to her amazing breasts and hips, making her look far older than her eighteen years. Her hair and makeup had been professionally styled and applied in a salon that afternoon. Her nails too. Fingers and toes.

He knew all of that because Jackson had grumbled about girls and their expensive needs earlier in the day. Rock knew her brother adored her, even though he never missed an opportunity to torment her.

Rock also knew Lyla was extremely low maintenance. If she wanted to take one day to doll herself up and go to a fancy prom, she deserved it. Hell, she'd earned it. She'd made straight A's all through school, gotten into an amazing university, and never caused her parents a single moment of worry.

She caused Rock, on the other hand, all kinds of worry. He'd spent the past two years keeping an eye on her, mostly to make sure no stupid boys gave her any trouble.

Luckily he'd never had to punch anyone in the face. Lyla never dated. She was shy and often preferred to be alone with her sketchpad and her books. He knew she thought she was invisible, but she was wrong. He certainly noticed her.

And he was noticing her now more than ever. After letting his gaze slide up her body from her dainty silver heels to the exposed cleavage of her dress, he cleared his throat. "You're going to have to hike your skirt up to your hips, Baby girl."

She bit into the bottom corner of her lip and shifted her weight back and forth. Every time she bit that lip—and it was often—his cock got hard.

He leaned the bike on the kickstand, stepped toward her, palmed her cheek, and used his thumb to dislodge her lip. "Stop that," he whispered. "You have no idea what that does to me."

She gasped, her eyes adorably wide.

He turned and opened his saddlebag to pull out a spare helmet. When he grabbed it, he also accidentally wrapped his fingers around the fluffy paw of the teddy bear at the bottom of the bag.

Rock rarely opened this bag. He rarely needed the spare helmet. He hadn't thought about the teddy bear in the bottom in a long time. Every member of his MC carried one just in case they encountered a damsel in distress. In the case of the Shadowridge Guardians MC, the damsel would most likely be a Little girl. Not someone young but a full-grown adult who liked to be nurtured and cared for.

He hesitated before turning around. There was no way in hell Lyla had any knowledge of age play or Daddy Doms. Though she'd given him submissive vibes and tendencies for the past two years, she was far too innocent and ignorant about the fetish community.

She was, however, an adult. Judging by the tears and sadness he'd seen in her eyes, she was also a damsel in distress. *What the hell? Why not?*

Turning around, Rock held out the stuffed bear. "Hold this for me, Little Lyla."

She tentatively reached out and took it before bringing it to her chest. "Why do you have a stuffed animal in your saddle-bag, Rock?" she asked while he settled the helmet over her hair.

He hated that he was ruining her expensive hairdo, but it was late. She surely would have taken it down soon anyway.

He shrugged, trying to be nonchalant as he fastened the buckle under her chin. "Never know when you might need a teddy bear." His gaze was on her lips, and he loved the way she slowly smiled.

"You're full of surprises tonight."

"Yep." *More than you can imagine.*

Granted, he had no thoughts about getting her naked. Not a chance in hell. She probably hadn't ever been kissed let alone fucked. He absolutely wasn't going to go down that path.

What the fuck are *you doing then, asshole?*

Okay, maybe he had *thought* about doing every imaginable dirty thing to her, but he'd never acted on it, and he wouldn't tonight either. Nope.

"You gonna pull that skirt up, Baby girl, or do you want me to do it?"

Her breath hitched as she reached down and shimmied the skin-tight material up her legs until it was gathered just below her pussy.

Rock held his breath as he climbed onto his bike. He patted

the seat behind him. "Have you ever ridden before, Baby girl?" He knew she hadn't. Hell, her parents would probably have a fit if they knew this was happening.

Ward and June Cleaver were polite people who tolerated Rock, but even after two years of friendship with their son, they still eyed him skeptically. Rock was pretty sure the only reason they'd welcomed him into their home at all in the beginning was because they suspected Rock was the reason Jackson was passing calculus. They weren't wrong.

Lyla shook her head. "I have on heels and this dress is totally inappropriate."

"You'll be fine." He pointed to the rung just behind him. "Put your foot there and swing over. Don't take your feet off the rungs while I'm driving."

This entire unplanned scenario had his dick harder than he could ever remember. His girl—okay, she wasn't his girl at all and never had been, but he'd thought of her as *his* for two years—was standing next to his bike with her dress hiked up, her tits tormenting him, and that damn teddy bear clutched in her arms.

His heart nearly stopped when she planted her left foot and grabbed his shoulders to swing her other leg over. And it skipped a beat entirely when she tucked the bear between them, flattened her front to his back, and set her hands on his hips.

"I'm scared. What if I fall off?" There was a tremor in her voice.

He grabbed her hands and pulled them all the way around his middle. "You won't fall, Baby girl. I'd never let that happen. Hold on tight. Don't let go. When I lean one way or the other, lean with me."

When he fired up the engine, she nearly jumped off the seat. "*Oh*," she exclaimed with no filter as she used her thighs to keep her cute ass suspended above the leather.

Fuck. Me.

His only reaction was a smirk over his shoulders. "Yeah. Now you know why chicks dig bikes." With that, he took off, leaving her posh neighborhood.

CHAPTER
THREE

I can't believe this is happening.

Lyla held on to Rock for dear life. She was both scared and invigorated. She'd thought about riding into the sunset with him a million times, but she'd never seriously expected it to happen.

Granted, it certainly wasn't sunset. It was nearly midnight. She'd certainly never envisioned herself riding behind him in a prom dress and heels. And, perhaps most important, she'd had no idea what the vibration of his bike would do to her pussy.

She realized she had no clue where he lived, and she didn't care. She never wanted this ride to end. She inhaled his scent, let the wind hit her in the face, and grinned from ear to ear.

Fifteen minutes ago, she'd been a hot mess of nerves. Rock had blown everything that had happened tonight right out of the stratosphere. Fuck her prom date and his cronies. The guy was a dick. He didn't deserve to occupy another moment of her headspace.

When Rock pulled into an apartment complex, Lyla found herself disappointed. She'd rather stay on this bike all night. Instead, she had to face the next phase in this crazy idea.

Rock parked, turned off the bike, and twisted to lift her up over the seat and set her on the ground. He didn't release her hips too quickly either. "You steady, Little Lyla?"

She took a second and nodded. It seemed like her legs would hold her up, even though they were noodles, and she was wearing heels. She quickly shimmied and tugged the dress until it fell back into place around her legs. While he dismounted, she tucked the bear under her arm, unfastened the helmet, then handed it to him when he turned around.

"My hair must look like I went through a hurricane." She reached up with her free hand to touch the curls that had tumbled from the top all evening. She held one of the stuffed bear's legs in her other hand.

Rock stowed both helmets and faced her. "Your hair is gorgeous, Baby girl. Don't fret." He took her hand and led her toward the building.

"These apartments look brand new," she commented.

"Yeah. They're nice. I'm glad I managed to get a unit."

"How long have you lived here?" It seemed awkward that she'd never asked where he lived. She was embarrassed now to realize she didn't know much about his life.

It was as if he were simply her brother's hot friend who materialized out of nowhere every once in a while and made her life a little sunnier. He did that without knowing it. He did it by looking at her with his smoldering gaze and speaking to her in his sultry voice. She was certain he had no idea.

When they reached the stairs, Rock turned toward her, bent at the knees, and swooped her off the ground to cradle her in his arms.

"*Rock*," she squealed. "What are you doing?"

"Baby girl, you are so wobbly on those sexy heels, I'm afraid you might fall on the stairs. And then I'd have to take you to the hospital and face your parents to explain how you broke your leg in the middle of the night at my apartment. I'm not up for that tonight." His voice was teasing.

Fine. If he was going to carry her, she was going to milk this strange night for every drop. She wrapped her arms around his neck and leaned her head on his shoulder.

Once again, she reminded herself he surely didn't see her as more than his friend's kid sister, but he didn't know what was happening in her head. Her fantasies were none of his business.

When they reached the door to his apartment, he jostled her easily to one side a bit and pulled the keys out of his pocket. He didn't set her down as he opened the door, nor did he set her down after he entered the apartment.

Rock Monroe carried her straight through the masculine living room and into the kitchen. Finally, he sat her on the counter next to the fridge.

She swayed slightly, feeling lightheaded from the shock of everything that was happening.

He planted his hands on the counter on both sides of her, crowding her and trapping her. "What would you like to drink, Baby girl?"

She licked her lips. What was the right answer? What did this tattooed sexy man even have to drink in his apartment? "Uh, beer?"

He laughed before grabbing her waist and shaking his head. "Not a snowball's chance in hell, Little girl. Have you ever even tried beer?"

She shook her head as her face heated.

"Have you ever tried any alcohol?"

She looked down. She was a goody two-shoes, and everyone knew it, including Rock. She didn't break rules or curfew. She was a perfect student. Even in her art, she never colored outside the lines.

He lifted her chin with a finger. "I'm sorry I laughed. You probably didn't need that. I'm a complex guy. My fridge has more than beer in it, Baby girl. How about lemon-lime soda or apple juice?"

Shocked by his choices, she asked, "Do you not drink caffeine?"

"Sure I do. I have several types of colas too, but Little girls don't need caffeine this late at night."

Her cheeks heated again. That was three times he'd called her a Little girl. He'd started calling her Little Lyla the day she'd met him. The nickname had never bothered her. It was their thing. He never said it in front of other people. It made her feel special, like she meant something to him. It made her feel cherished.

But Little girl?

"I'm not a baby, you know." She straightened her spine and stared at him. "In fact, I'm not a child at all. I'm eighteen now."

"Baby girl, I've never been more aware of anything in my life as I am about your age and your adult status. That's not going to stop me from calling you Little girl. It's in my blood. I'm a nurturing guy by nature. My instinct is to take care of you and make sure you're safe."

"Oh." Her head was spinning. Half of his words didn't make much sense to her, and the other half made her panties wet. What did he mean by being overly aware of her age?

"How about if I choose for you?" he suggested. Keeping one hand extended across her body and planted on the counter as if to keep her from falling, he used the other to pull the fridge open.

She didn't look inside. She didn't want to take her gaze off him. How long would he let her stay here? How many hours was this most perfect night of her life going to last?

When she saw the drink he'd pulled out, she giggled. "Why do you have juice boxes in your fridge?"

He shrugged as he put the straw in the hole. "Never hurts to be prepared. Never know when the prettiest Little girl in the world might come by and need a drink."

She took the juice box from him and sipped down most of it in one long drink. "I guess I was thirsty."

"There's plenty more. Help yourself if you want another or ask me to get it for you."

"'K."

He pushed back a few inches and surprised her again when he lifted one of her feet and removed the shoe. He did the same to the other side before setting the stilettos on the floor next to the cabinets. "I bet your toes were screaming."

"Yeah. They kind of were."

"How much dancing did you do?"

She shrugged and looked away. "Not much," she muttered. "I don't really want to talk about the dance, Rock. Can't we just pretend it didn't happen and move on?"

"Nope. I want to hear the details. I want to know what happened to make you arrive home alone with tears in your eyes. Do I need to hunt down the boy you went to prom with and teach him some manners?"

She gasped, eyes going wide.

Rock snickered. "Baby girl, unless that boy did something worthy of a good hard lesson, I'm kidding."

"Oh." Shrugging as if she hadn't totally taken him seriously, she continued, "I mean it's not a bad idea."

Rock drew in a breath. "Start from the beginning." He scooped her off the counter, handed her the bear she'd placed next to the sink, and made sure she had a grip on her juice box. "Let's go sit on the couch."

As he deposited her on the sectional, she squirmed to adjust her dress. It was hard to sit comfortably in the damn thing. It was made for standing. Not even walking. The skirt had kept her from taking more than baby steps.

Rock leaned over her, setting both hands on the back of the sofa, pinning her in the way he'd done on the kitchen counter. "You're uncomfortable. That dress is sexy as fuck but you've had enough of it, haven't you?"

Her breath hitched. Had he just said she was sexy?

"You heard me, Little Lyla. And don't act so surprised. You

spent all day getting ready for the prom. At least four people worked on you, doing your hair and makeup and nails. Am I wrong?"

She shook her head.

"So yeah, sexy as fuck. Don't ever doubt it. But I bet you'd like to get out of that dress. How about if I lend you one of my T-shirts? It would hang low enough to keep you fully covered."

"What if I don't want to be fully covered?" she blurted before she could filter her thoughts. She slapped a hand over her mouth, mortified.

Rock groaned. "Baby girl... Don't tempt me. You've been legal for like a minute. I'm not going to take advantage of you. I just want to make you comfortable."

She glanced at his black-T-shirt-covered chest as she lowered her hand, feeling feisty and flirtatious. So out of her element. "Can I have the one you're wearing?"

The groan that came from between his lips made her squeeze her legs together. She was going to self-combust. In addition, she was pretty sure he knew it.

Lyla had secrets. Sure, she presented herself as a total prude with her conservative clothes, high work ethic, and rule-following, but when she was alone in her bedroom at night, she let herself go into her fantasy mode.

Sometimes she read smutty books. Other times she simply closed her eyes and visualized every imaginable scenario with Rock. She liked to pretend he was her man. Meanwhile, she'd grown exceptionally capable of getting herself off with her fingers.

Rock stepped back, grabbed her hand, and pulled her to her feet. "Turn around."

She spun away from him and held her breath while he lowered the zipper all the way down her back before turning her to face him once again. Releasing her, he hauled his T-shirt over his head and handed it to her. "Change, Baby girl."

She was reeling as he spun around.

Oh. He means here. Now. Take off the dress and put his shirt on.

Jesus, this was hot. Why was this so hot? Probably because everything Rock did was hot all the time.

Lyla dropped the dress, stepped out of the pile of silk, and hauled the T-shirt over her head. She even lifted the front of it to her nose to savor his scent.

"You good?"

"Yes." She sat, tucked her legs up under her, settled the bear in her lap, and held on to him, hoping he would provide moral support and courage. She didn't care if Rock judged her for keeping the bear close. Besides, he'd given it to her. What did he expect her to do?

The teddy bear felt like a lifeline, grounding her in the present.

CHAPTER
FOUR

You've lost your mind, Monroe. What the hell are you doing?

Rock had not planned this. None of it. He'd waited for Lyla to get home for peace of mind. He hadn't been certain he would even approach her. He'd waited on the basement steps for an hour, expecting her to come in smiling and giddy from her big dance.

When she'd stepped into the kitchen with her shoulders drooping and head hung, he'd quietly risen to his feet. When she'd sniffled, he'd lost it. Who the fuck had hurt her and why?

Rock lowered himself onto the couch next to her, not giving her any space. He let his thigh touch her knee, twisted so he was more fully facing her, and set his arm behind her on the back of the couch.

Picking up one of the tendrils of hair at the base of her neck, he fingered it. "Tell me what happened, Little Lyla."

She sighed. "I'd rather not. It's embarrassing. Can't we just sit here and not talk?"

He met her gaze. Her eyes were watery again. Something

happened tonight to upset her, and he didn't like it. "Was it that punk Casper?"

She gave him a small smile when he fucked up the name again. "Aspen."

"Right. Aspen." He rolled his eyes. "Who names their kid Aspen?"

She shrugged and looked down at the bear, plucking at his fur absentmindedly.

"Aspen's a decent name for a stuffed bear," Rock suggested as he rested his hand on top of hers.

She lifted her gaze, her face scrunched up in a sneer. Now they were getting somewhere.

"No? What should we name him?"

"The bear? Or my shitty prom date? Asshole works for the prom date. I'm not sure I've ever named a stuffed animal."

Rock gasped dramatically. "You don't name your stuffies?"

She shook her head, giggling, causing the lock of hair to slip from his fingers.

Continuing to cup the back of her hand over the bear, he squeezed her fingers and leaned forward. "You'll hurt his feelings if you don't name him."

She giggled again. He loved it when she laughed. It was the sweetest sound in the world. When she looked down at the bear again, she asked, "Do I get to keep him?"

"Of course. I wouldn't take back a Little girl's bear."

"Then I'll name him Rock, and when I'm away at school this fall, I'll talk to him as if he's you, and he'll comfort me when I feel down."

A lump formed in Rock's throat, and he cupped the back of her head and pulled her closer so her cheek rested on his shoulder. "Do I? Comfort you when you're down?"

She nodded. "Always."

"Good. I'm glad." He stroked her neck and shoulders. "Now, I'm not going to ask again. Tell me what's making you feel down tonight."

She tipped her head back and looked up at him. "You say that like you're my parent, and you're going to spank me if I don't comply." Her voice was joking.

His cock grew harder. She was so damn close to the truth. *She has no clue, Monroe. Be careful.*

"Hmm. Would you like that? It might make you feel better. A good spanking on a Little girl's bottom can help erase stress and anxiety."

She slowly pushed back from him, holding his gaze. "You're serious." A shudder wracked her body. A good one, he hoped.

Careful, Monroe. "Yep. But first I want you to talk to me. Afterward, if you'd like me to spank you to chase away the icky feelings, I'll be happy to do so. If you don't start talking, you're going to end up over my knees for a naughty-girl spanking instead."

Rock watched her so closely, afraid to even blink. He didn't want to miss a single nuance of her reaction. He was treading on thin ice here. Breaking every boundary he'd intended to keep between them tonight.

He meant to comfort her. Not Daddy her. At least not in a way she would notice. Suddenly, he found himself holding his girl in his arms on his couch in his apartment. She was wearing his T-shirt over God-only-knew-what sexy scraps of lace. She was submitting to him in a way he'd only dreamed about. Her eyes were wide as saucers as she absorbed his words.

She licked those full lips again. "You're confusing me. You look at me like you want to undress me with your eyes. You're touching me like the woman I've always wanted you to see me as. But you're talking to me as though I was a child."

"Not a child, Little Lyla. Just someone who needs nurturing. There's a difference. I'm fully aware you're a grown adult now. That doesn't mean you don't crave being cared for by someone who worships the ground you walk on."

Her breath hitched and her lip trembled. She looked away again.

He wanted to pull her all the way onto his lap, but that would probably be a bad idea, and he still needed answers before anything else. "Did that Brinkman guy hurt you?"

She shook her head. "Only my pride. I'm pretty sure he only asked me to the prom on a bet. I'm also pretty sure I shocked him with my dress, hair, and makeup. I think I shocked the entire school." She lifted her gaze and grinned.

"Not surprising, Baby girl. You were smoking hot in that dress. I almost couldn't get my legs to hold me up when I saw you walk in the kitchen door. If I'd been there and seen you before you'd left, I might not have let you go."

Her eyes went wide again.

"Go on. I guess you drove yourself to the dance?"

She drew in a breath. "Yeah. That was my father's idea. He said, that way, I could easily leave any time I wanted. He was right. I met a group of people for dinner first. It went okay. Mostly the guys kept staring at my cleavage and the girls kept whispering to each other about me." She shrugged. "I'm used to it. I ignored them and ate my meal."

"Then what happened?"

"We went to the dance. Aspen barely paid attention to me. It was awkward and uncomfortable wandering around the dance hall by myself. I felt like everyone was staring at me and whispering."

"Probably because you're stunning and smart and funny and they're all jealous."

She rolled her eyes. "I don't think that's it, Rock."

"Their loss. Go on."

She drew in another breath. "When I decided to cut my losses and leave, I went in search of Aspen. I found him talking with two of his friends. They didn't see me approach. As I got closer, I realized they were talking about me."

Rock stiffened. "What did they say, Little Lyla?"

"Aspen said, 'Pay up. I got her here.' And then his friend said, 'If you're not going to tap that, you're crazy. How about if…' " Lyla lowered her face again, but not before Rock saw the tears sliding down her cheeks.

"Finish," Rock encouraged on a whisper. "Get it out." He lowered his hand and rubbed her back.

Her voice was choked with emotion. "How about if I take over. I'll let you know tomorrow how tight that virgin cunt was in the morning."

Rock stopped breathing. Those assholes. Jesus.

Throwing caution to the wind, he scooped her up and settled her on his lap, holding her tight as she sniffled. He kissed the top of her head. "I'm sorry, Baby girl. That was crude and uncalled for. Did you confront them?"

She shook her head and whimpered against his bare chest. "No, I turned and left the dance. I'm so glad I had a car."

"Me too, Little Lyla. Me too." He rocked her and kissed her temple several times. "It's over now. You're ten times more mature than any of those boys. Ten times more interesting and talented and smart. After school gets out next week, you'll never see those assholes again."

After a few minutes of silence, she tipped her head back again. "Did you mean it?"

"Mean what, Baby girl?"

"Would you really spank me to chase away the icky feelings?"

CHAPTER
FIVE

Lyla couldn't believe she'd just said that. She couldn't believe anything about this surreal night. She especially couldn't believe Rock seemed interested in her as more than just his friend's kid sister.

She had no idea when she might ever get a chance to experience something like this again. Perhaps never. So she wasn't going to let this opportunity slip away.

She'd had no idea Rock was such a kinky guy. Spanking? And why did the idea of him swatting her bottom make her panties wet?

Rock looked a bit stunned by her request, and she feared he might turn her down or tell her she'd misunderstood. Instead, he finally nodded. "If that's what you want, Baby girl," he said in a soft voice.

She nodded, and before she could lose her nerve, she asked, "Will you have sex with me, too?"

Rock's eyes shot wider than she'd ever seen them, and she wished she could take the question back. *He doesn't see you that way, you dimwit.*

Embarrassed beyond belief, she shoved at him to get off his lap. She needed to get out of here. She was mortified.

His grip tightened on her, and he held her fast. "Little girl, stop squirming around. Every time you move, your thigh rubs against my cock."

She gasped and attempted to twist away again. But wait… If she was affecting him that way…

Rock wrapped his arms all the way around her slim body and held her closer. "Don't panic," he whispered. "I'm not rejecting you. I'm just shocked. Give me a second to process what you just asked me."

She was breathing heavily as she stared down at his chest. This was the first time she'd seen him without a shirt on, and he was ripped. Plus, he had more tattoos than she'd known about. She knew he'd gotten several of them in the past two years since she'd met him.

"Forget I said anything," she pleaded.

He chuckled, which vibrated her entire body. "No man alive could possibly forget a woman asking him to have sex, Baby girl."

"You probably think I'm just some kid, your friend's little sister. A nuisance. You're just being nice to me because…" She lifted her gaze. "Why are you being nice to me?"

He set a finger under her chin and held her gaze. "Little Lyla, I have never for a second seen you as a nuisance, a kid, or anyone's sister. From the moment I met you, I've been adjusting my cock."

Her jaw fell open. "Why didn't you say anything?"

"You were too young, Baby girl. Your parents barely tolerate a guy like me as a friend of their son's. They would've had me arrested if I'd approached you."

"Oh." He had a point. She'd never thought about that before. She'd always just wondered why he seemed to follow her around the room with his gaze and why he went out of his way to be so nice to her. Finally, she gave him a coy smile. "I'm eighteen now."

He groaned. "Don't I know it." His hands slid to her lower

back. "I'm equally certain I'm probably an ass for bringing you here and even considering introducing you to my world."

She had no idea what he was talking about, but she wanted to know. "What world is that?"

"I'm a dominant, Lyla. I doubt you even know what that means."

She shot him a glare. "I'm a smart gal. I know what a dominant is. You mean you like to tie women up, blindfold them, and flog them. Stuff like that?" The idea made her nipples harder than they'd already been. Sheesh.

He swallowed hard. "Lord, you do know more than I gave you credit for. But no. I'm not that kind of dominant. I'm a Daddy Dom."

She furrowed her brow. "What's a Daddy Dom?"

"A man who likes to nurture and protect his Little girl. Someone who likes her to submit to his rules and guidelines to keep her safe and happy."

She tried to process his words. She'd never read anything about Daddy Doms. Now she wished she could put a pause on this conversation, freeze the world, and check out ten books from the library about the subject, if such books even existed. But that wasn't going to happen. Instead, she was going to have to ask questions.

She inhaled slowly. "What kinds of rules?"

"Things like not going out alone at night, not using knives without supervision, not running in the house, not cussing or talking back to Daddy. Things that keep a Little girl safe mostly."

She squirmed on his lap. Her panties were soaked by his tone and his serious manner. "How does not cussing keep me safe?"

He grinned. "It would keep your bottom from hurting when you sit down."

She squeezed her legs together at another mention of

spanking her. She needed more information. "Are there other people like that? Other Daddy Doms?"

"More than you can imagine. The Shadowridge Guardians MC has many members who practice some form of ageplay for example."

"Ageplay…"

"That's what we call relationships comprised of a Daddy and a Little girl." He patted her back. "And again, let me stress, the term Little girl or Baby girl refers to an adult woman who enters into a relationship with a Daddy Dom with full consent and knowledge."

Lyla nodded slowly. It was a lot to absorb. She shifted back to his original pronouncement about being a Dominant. "So you don't want to tie me up and blindfold me?"

He chuckled. "If that was something you craved, I could certainly do so. Lots of people enjoy some form of restraint when they have sex. They like feeling as though they don't have control over their own pleasure."

Lyla flinched when he tipped his head back and groaned. "How the hell did we get into this deep discussion? You're so green and, fuck, probably a virgin."

"Is that a problem?"

He dropped his forehead to hers. "No. Jesus, Lyla, no. Not a problem. It's a *fact*, and I'm not sure it would be fair of me to take your virginity in the middle of the night while you're so emotional and I've just dropped a few dozen bombs on your lap about my sexual preferences."

She sat up straighter. "But that's my decision." Time to fill him in on a few other *facts*. "I've lusted over you for two years. I've spent countless hours wondering what it would be like to have sex with you. You're going to leave town for your internship in a few days, and I'm going away to college this fall. I want my first time to be with *you*. Please don't make me beg."

He stared at her for several seconds before smoothing his giant hands up her back and back down to cup her butt over the T-shirt. "Okay, Baby girl. Let's start with the spanking and see how you feel afterward."

He lifted her off his lap and stood her in front of him. "Turn around and kneel in front of me, Baby girl. I want to pull these pins out of your hair. That hairdo can't possibly be comfortable anymore."

He was right. Her head was starting to throb. The thought of him taking it all down made her nipples stiffen again. She crossed her arms to hide the reaction, even though he surely couldn't see her tight buds through her lace bra and the loose black T-shirt.

If she kneeled in front of him and let him play with her hair, she would end up moaning so loudly she'd embarrass herself. The visualization nearly made her orgasm.

"I can do it," she whispered as she lifted her hands to the curls. She would need a mirror and probably half an hour, to be honest.

Rock wrapped his hands around her wrists and gently lowered them to her sides. "It's the kind of thing Daddies like to do. Fix their Little girl's hair. Comb it. Wash it. Braid it."

She swallowed. This was the oddest conversation she'd ever had in her life, and she was so intrigued she wanted to shout: *Yes, please. Do all those things.* "Okay," she whispered.

He lifted her hands to his lips and kissed her knuckles. "Okay, Daddy," he corrected.

She shuddered. A full-body shudder that left her knees weak and her body heated. "Okay, Daddy," she responded.

He gave her the brightest smile she'd ever seen. "I love the sound of that, Baby girl. Now turn around and let Daddy take your hair down."

She did as she was told, grateful when he dropped a throw pillow onto the floor between his feet. He spread his knees and helped her kneel in front of him, letting his knees slide under her arms.

"How many of these pins are there, Little Lyla?" he teased as he started deftly pulling them out.

She giggled. "I don't know. A million?"

His deep chuckle rumbled against her where his knees gripped her sides. He was so careful pulling each pin out that he never once made her wince.

"You're good at that," she murmured as she let her eyes slide closed so she could enjoy the feel of his hands in her hair.

Eventually, he had them all out, and he carefully finger-combed her hair down around her shoulders. "You weren't kidding about the shellac, Little girl. This hair was nearly glued in place."

"Maybe you could wash it for me after you ravage me," she suggested, uncertain who had taken over her body and turned her into a sex-starved nymph.

His responding groan pleased her immensely as he helped her to her feet. "One thing at a time, Baby girl. You're killing me."

She grinned as she stepped between his legs, leaned against him, and wrapped her arms around his neck. "Please don't die on me. I have a list of experiences I'd like to check off before the sun comes up."

Standing like this between his legs put their faces at nearly the same level, and Rock looked like he was going to devour her for a few seconds before he grabbed the back of her head and did exactly that.

His lips landed on hers with more passion than she'd ever imagined. He didn't just kiss her; he consumed her. He destroyed her. With a kiss.

He angled her head how he wanted it seconds later, licked along the seam of her lips to demand entrance, and slid his tongue in to dance with hers.

Moans filled the room, and she had no idea which of them they were coming from. Probably both. Her knees grew weak, but when she started to buckle, he tucked a hand under her butt and held her up.

Time stood still while she enjoyed every moment of this kiss. For a fleeting moment, she remembered those stupid boys discussing her earlier in the evening, and she smirked inside, knowing none of them would ever have been able to kiss her like this.

When Rock finally broke free, he didn't go far. He continued to hold her close, panting and staring into her eyes with pure lust. "Jesus, Little Lyla."

A flush crawled up her cheeks. "Did I do it right?" *He* certainly had, but she had no idea if she measured up.

"Do it right?" His voice rose. "If you'd done it any more *right*, I would have come in my jeans. Was that your first kiss, Baby girl?"

She nodded, embarrassed to admit her total inexperience.

He moaned and kissed her again, briefly this time. "I'm going to steal all your firsts tonight. You ready for that, Baby girl?"

She nodded. "Yes, Daddy." It surprised her how easily the word slid from her tongue. Half an hour ago she'd never considered calling a lover *Daddy*, and here she was using it flippantly like it was totally normal.

The steamy look in his eyes told her he loved it.

CHAPTER
SIX

Rock was going to self-combust. She was beyond perfection. He'd imagined a scenario like this a million times over the past two years, but he'd never expected to be able to pile all this information on her in one hour and have her staring at him with those deep brown, sexy, please-fuck-me eyes.

His girl had barely flinched as he'd filled her in on his sexual preferences. She was eager and willing and leaning against him, begging to be ravished.

Was he making a mistake? God, he hoped not. If she'd shown any signs of wanting to run screaming from the apartment, he would have taken her home and kept his hands to himself. But that wasn't what had happened. Not by a long shot.

And damn. He was completely incapable of denying his girl what she wanted. He'd never be able to tell her *no* in his entire life.

The thought made him stiffen. What happened after tonight? He was leaving. When he got back, she would be gone. She needed to go to college, follow her dreams, get her degree. He would never suggest she give that up.

Nope. They would have to figure this out as they went along. For now, he had tonight, and he intended to make the most of it.

Easing her back, he guided her to one side. "Lie across my lap, Baby girl. Daddy is going to spank your bottom and chase away all the bad feelings from earlier."

She was trembling as she let him help her into position across his thighs. She was nervous, but he would take his time and watch her closely. With one hand on the small of her back, he patted the backs of her thighs with the other, easing his fingers closer to her bottom. "I'll start easy, Little Lyla. Let you get used to the feeling. If you want me to stop at any time, just say *red*, okay?"

"Yes, Daddy." Her voice was breathy, but every time she called him Daddy, his cock jumped. This was every dream he'd ever had wrapped up in one.

Rock held his breath as he pushed his T-shirt up her body until he slid the cotton under his palm at the small of her back. It took all his self-control not to flip her over and plant his face between her legs when he saw the fucking sexy black thong.

He rubbed her bare cheeks. "You naughty Little girl. That's some seriously sexy lingerie."

She shivered. "I couldn't wear regular panties with that dress. Someone would have seen the lines. The sales lady sold me this bra and thong set when I bought the dress."

"Do you have other panties like this at home, Baby girl?" Why he needed to know that he had no idea, but he wanted to visualize what she normally wore under her jeans and dresses.

She shook her head. "No. Just these," she whispered.

"Tell me what you normally wear, Little Lyla." He needed to know. He couldn't explain why.

"Just regular bikini panties. Pastel mostly."

He stared at her fantastic ass while he pictured her in those pastel panties. He'd give anything to be the one to put them on her in the mornings. That wasn't going to happen anytime soon, but he'd think about it every day.

After hooking his finger under the edge of the black lace, he slowly drew the thong over her bottom, down her thighs, and off.

She shuddered.

"When I spank you, it will always be on your bare bottom, Baby girl. I'll want to keep a close eye on your skin to make sure it turns hot and pink without bruising." He rubbed her perfect globes again. He could do this all night. Removing the thong hadn't been entirely necessary. It hadn't been covering her fantastic ass cheeks, but he'd wanted them off her anyway.

She whimpered and squirmed on his lap.

"Spread your legs for me, Little Lyla."

Her breathing picked up as she complied, opening her thighs a few inches.

"Good girl. I don't want you to clench your legs together while I'm spanking you." He lifted his hand and gave her a firm swat. Just hard enough to sting and surprise her.

She flinched, but the sound that came out of her mouth was musical.

He did it again. Jesus, she was responsive, and he'd bet his last dollar her pussy was soaked. He intended to find out soon. Would she have curls there or would she be bare? When he leaned to the side to see between her legs better, he saw no evidence of hair.

He continued to spank her several more times, grateful he'd not only seen this done many times among club members, but he'd practiced on a few of the old ladies who enjoyed a good spanking. It had never been sexual with any of them, though. This was definitely sexual. Not just for him, but for Lyla.

When he paused to rub her heated skin and check on her, she was panting. "Rock…"

"Daddy," he reminded her. "Especially when you're over my knees, Baby girl."

"Sorry, Daddy."

"More, Little Lyla?"

"Please," she murmured, as if it was difficult to admit.

He kept his palm spread solidly on her lower back so she couldn't squirm off his lap and onto the floor. The way she was wiggling told him she'd probably enjoy restraints. Little girls, who squirmed during a spanking like Lyla was, were usually silently begging to have their movements constrained.

He spanked her a dozen more times, watching her closely and stopping when she arched her back and lifted her legs. There was a good chance she was close to orgasm.

While she was totally off balance, he slid his hand from the back of her knee up to her pussy, coming just shy of touching her. Easing the last inch or so until he could barely stroke over her folds, his heart nearly stopped when he found her not only soaked but bare.

And the noise she made…

"Has anyone ever touched this sweet pussy, Little Lyla?"

She shook her head.

"What about you? Do you play with your pretty pussy when you're alone?" He reached between her folds and dragged his finger through the wetness. Fuck, she was killing him. "Answer Daddy, Baby girl. Do you touch yourself?"

"Yes, Daddy."

"Can you make yourself come with your fingers, Lyla?"

Another whimper. "Yes, Daddy," she whispered.

"What do you think about when you're under the covers late at night playing with this sweet pussy?"

She moaned but didn't respond fast enough.

He removed his fingers and gripped her bottom hard enough to bring attention to the burn. "Answer Daddy, Baby girl." He knew the answer. He wanted to hear her say it. He *needed* to hear her say it even if he came in his pants.

"You, Daddy," she blurted. "I think of you. Please…"

He needed to be inside her more than his next breath. But not here. Not on the couch. This wasn't where he was going to thrust into his precious Little girl for the first time.

Grabbing her around the waist, he rose to his feet. "Wrap your legs around me, Baby girl."

She complied, her wet pussy up high enough to rub directly against his belly. She even hooked her ankles together and ground herself against him.

Killing me.

Rock wasted no time getting to his bedroom where he aimed directly for his bed and lowered her onto her back. Her legs were still hooked around him as he grabbed the hem of his shirt and pushed it up her body and over her head. He dragged it higher, forcing her arms together above her head.

Standing on the floor between her legs, he grabbed the tangle of cotton and tied a giant knot in it between her wrists. It forced her hands together and essentially restrained her. "Leave your hands here, Baby girl."

Her eyes were wide, and she was breathing heavily as he kissed the spot between her breasts before dragging his tongue along the edge of the lace.

She arched her chest and moaned. "Daddy…"

Fucking heaven.

Grateful for the front clasp on her bra, he made quick work of popping it open to reveal the tits he'd dreamed about for two fucking years.

Gorgeous. Jesus. Stunning. Her nipples were rosy points begging for attention, and he bent his head and flicked his tongue over first one and then the other.

She arched and bucked and squirmed and moaned.

"Such a wiggly Little girl." He cupped both breasts and molded his fingers around them before flicking the nipples with his thumbs and finally pinching them both lightly.

"Oh. God…"

"Do you enjoy nipple play, Little Lyla? Do you like to pinch these tight buds while you finger your pussy?" He was being so crude. He'd never dreamed she'd be ready for this kind of dirty talk, but she wasn't like other women. She was so sexual and needy.

She nodded. "Yes," she whispered. "Not too hard, though. It feels better when you tap them or graze over them."

Damn. He loved that she was able and willing to verbalize her needs. So fucking sensual. So far beyond her years for a virgin.

Rock listened to her and touched her the way she liked, teasing the little buds until she was writhing and losing her mind with need. "Let your legs fall open, Baby girl."

She complied, spreading herself wide for him.

He kissed a path down her belly until he reached her pussy. Holding her thighs parted, he set his gaze on her pussy for the first time.

There were no words for how pretty she was or how wet or how greedy. "Did you shave this pussy tonight? Or do you keep it bare all the time?" He trailed a finger along her folds, tormenting her to the point that he had to hold her down with his other hand on her pelvis.

Lyla dug her heels into the mattress and tried to lift her pussy right off the bed.

He removed his fingers. He loved the way he could get her to talk by withdrawing contact. "Answer Daddy," he encouraged again. He knew she was having trouble focusing, but he wanted her to spill all her secrets.

She whimpered, rolling her head back and forth. "I've been shaving it for a while. I like how it feels," she murmured. "Please touch me, Daddy."

He trailed a finger around her clit, watching her face. "You've thought about this, haven't you? You've thought about me touching your bare little pussy and making you scream."

"Yes. A million times. Yes," she cried out. "It's so much better in real life."

"Oh, Baby girl. You have no idea. I haven't even gotten started yet." He lowered his head and sucked her clit into his mouth.

Lyla screamed. The most beautiful sound in the world.

Rock flicked his tongue over her captive clit as rapidly as possible as he eased one finger into her tight channel. That was all it took. Her orgasm had been building for an hour. It was a wonder she'd lasted this long. The sound and feel of her coming on his mouth and finger brought him to his knees.

While she was still panting and twitching, he added a second finger. Damn, she was tight. "So gorgeous. Prettiest Little girl in the world. Tell Daddy what's been up inside this precious little cunt, Baby girl."

She shuddered, still moaning through the orgasm. Finally, she licked her lips. "My fingers, tampons, and... stuff."

"Stuff?" His curiosity was piqued. "What stuff, Little Lyla?" Dragging information from her was his new favorite pastime. He loved how her cheeks turned pink with embarrassment.

She groaned. "Daddy..." She drew her restrained hands down to cover her eyes.

He reached up and pulled them back above her head and looked her in the eye, waiting with nothing more than a look.

She sighed heavily. "I have a set of thick markers I use for art class. They probably aren't nearly as big as your, uh... as you. But I pretend."

"My cock," he teased, grinning at her. "I don't think they make markers the size of my cock, Baby girl, but I give you kudos for the creativity." She was so precious.

"Maybe you could take your pants off and show me."

"You're sure that's what you want? There's no going back. We don't have to have sex just because you're naked in my apartment."

She rolled her eyes. "Stop stalling. I'm ready."

He stood and watched her face as he popped the button on his jeans before lowering them and his underwear over his hips.

She bit her lip, stifling her gasp.

He shrugged out of the denim, leaving himself naked. With his cock bobbing demandingly in front of him, he yanked open the drawer next to his bed and snagged the box of condoms.

Damn. He wished he'd opened the box earlier. His hands were shaking as he tore into the cellophane and tossed it aside before ripping the cardboard nearly down the center.

"That's a new box…" she commented.

He flinched as he snagged one of the foil packs and looked her in the eye.

"Why is the box new?"

"I'm not a virgin, if that's what you're wondering, Little Lyla, but I'm not a manwhore either. I don't bring women to my apartment. You're the first one."

Her eyes were wide again. He loved shocking her. "Oh."

He braced his hands on either side of her and lowered his face closer to hers. "You're not a conquest, Lyla. You mean something to me. I hope you know that."

She nodded slowly. "Okay."

Rising back to standing, he stroked his cock from base to tip while he tore the foil packet open with his teeth. "How many markers am I?"

She swallowed. "At least three, Daddy."

He grinned.

"It's going to hurt. I know that. I've heard other girls talking about it. It's okay, you know. I'll be fine."

He rolled the condom on and cupped her face. "You're right. It will burn for a minute, but you'll adjust around me, and then it will feel so good."

She licked her lips. "You won't be disappointed if it

doesn't, though, right? I mean other girls talk like it's a chore they don't really care for. They do it for their boyfriends."

He couldn't keep from smirking. "That's not going to happen. I'll never do anything to you that you don't thoroughly enjoy, Baby girl. I don't even like the idea of hurting you with my cock this first time, but it's part of nature. I can't help it. I promise you're not going to be disappointed. Those girls you hear talking are having sex with greedy boys who don't care about them. They only care about themselves and getting their rocks off. You mean far more to me than that."

"Okay," she whispered.

He knew she had her doubts, but all he could do was prove himself. And he fully intended to.

CHAPTER
SEVEN

Lyla was trembling as she stared at Rock's hard body and his enormous erection. No wonder girls spoke of sex with a grimace. He was crazy if he thought she was going to enjoy having that put inside her, but it had to happen at some point, and she wanted it to be him.

Her body was limp from the amazing orgasm he'd given her. It had blown the doors off every other orgasm she'd given herself. By a longshot.

"Can I have my hands, Daddy? I want to be able to touch you."

He reached above her and tugged the shirt free. "There. Are you going to leave marks on my back that will cause all the guys at the club to make fun of me if I take my shirt off?"

"Maybe?" She shrugged. She'd dreamed of making marks on him with her fingernails. "Will you be mad?"

"Fuck no. Never. I'll wear them with pride." He tucked his hands under her arms and dragged her to the center of the bed so he could climb up with her and nestle between her legs.

She grabbed his shoulders and held her breath, thinking he would thrust into her now.

But he didn't. Instead, he lowered his lips to hers and

kissed her like he had earlier, like he was dying of thirst and she was his tall glass of water. By the time he broke free, his erection was lodged at her entrance.

"You can still say no, Little Lyla."

She shook her head. "Do it, Daddy. Show me."

He clearly gritted his teeth as he eased partway into her.

Fuck. He was so big. Too big. She gripped his shoulders firmly, trying not to react.

Rock pulled almost out before entering again, slightly deeper.

Her lip quivered uncontrollably. "Daddy?"

He froze. "Want me to stop, Baby girl?" His voice was strained.

"No. I want you to just do it. Please. Stop teasing. Thrust all the way in."

He inhaled through his nose and lowered his forehead to hers. He gripped her face with both hands and thrust all the way in.

Lyla gasped. Her vision swam. *Jesus. Fuck.* Too big. Too big.

"Take a breath, Baby girl."

She shook her head in his hands. There was no way she was going to breathe. Maybe never again.

"Lyla…" he warned. "Take a breath for Daddy. Relax your body. Let your cunt adjust to my cock. You're clenching me so hard you're strangling my dick."

That last part was said in jest, but she couldn't smile. She did manage to draw in a deep lungful of air and release it.

"Good girl. Again."

She would never be able to disobey him if he was going to talk to her like that. She loved the way she felt when he called her his *good girl*.

After another breath, she loosened her grip on his shoulders.

He kissed her. First her lips, then all over her face. Finally, he eased partway out and back in.

She stiffened, but it didn't hurt like the first time.

He did it again.

Nerve endings she hadn't known existed came to life.

The next time, she whimpered and lifted her hips to meet him.

"That's my good girl. Let it feel good. Let your body accept me."

Languidly, he eased in and out while her arousal grew. When he lowered one hand to tease her nipple before wedging it between their bodies until he found her clit, she moaned.

Holy shit.

"That's my girl. So precious. So pretty. So fucking sexy." He kissed her again as he rubbed her clit.

She felt another orgasm building, stunning her. At the realization she might actually come again, she started bucking against him, loving the way he filled her and how the base of his penis rubbed against her with every pass. Even with his fingers between them she could feel his pelvis making contact with hers.

"Come around my cock, Baby girl. Come all over me before I release."

His words did something to her. He had an odd ability to command her to do things, and this was no exception. Her orgasm slammed into her, sending her flying. The pulses of her release were so much more powerful with her channel wrapped around his erection.

"Jesus, Little Lyla. Fuck me." Rock thrust several more times, faster now, with urgency and a driving need. It was so sexy watching him unravel. When he came with a loud grunt, his eyes rolled back and his mouth dropped open.

His entire body jerked with every squirt of his semen into the condom.

He was truly the most gorgeous man alive.

CHAPTER
EIGHT

Rock wrapped his arms around Lyla and rolled her to one side, managing to keep himself lodged inside her. He tucked one leg over her hips to keep her from escaping while he kissed her.

When he ran out of steam, he dropped his head next to hers, tucked a lock of hair behind her ear, and held her gaze. He knew he was grinning from ear to ear. "Were they right?" he asked in a gravelly voice.

"Who?" she whispered, her fingers trailing across his shoulder.

"The girls at school who said sex was a chore?"

Her face pinkened adorably. "Uh, no. They need to try a better man."

He chuckled and cupped her face. "How did I get so lucky?"

She shrugged. "I was thinking the same thing."

He lifted his face to glance at the clock. "What time do you think you need to be home?"

"Never. Take me away. Let's go to the Bahamas or someplace warm with a beach where I can waltz around all day in a bikini and tempt you with my feminine wiles."

He laughed. "Sounds like heaven, but it's not very practical."

She sighed dramatically. "Fine." She stuck out her bottom lip in a pout. "I want to stay a few more hours, though. Is that okay? Do you need to be somewhere in the morning?"

"I wouldn't care if I had a fourteen-hour shift that started at seven and I got no sleep. I'm going to steal every single second with you and then box them up so I can pull them out and relive this night over and over while you're halfway across the country from me."

"Maybe going to college is overrated?"

He rose onto an elbow and stared down at her. "Little girl, do not talk like that. You need to get your degree and follow your dreams."

"But…"

He covered her lips with his fingers. "No buts. Listen to your Daddy. Let's not talk about tomorrow. I want my few more hours to be blissful. I want to create memories. Let's take a shower."

She grinned wide. "Are you going to wash my hair?"

"I'm going to wash your entire body, Baby girl. And then you're going to wash mine. And then I'm going to spread you out like a feast on this bed and eat your pussy until you scream again."

She flushed. "Is that so?"

"Yep."

"What about me? Do I get to suck your cock until you come against the back of my throat?"

He flinched at the visual. "Jesus, Little Lyla, where did that dirty mouth come from?"

She shrugged. "Bad language doesn't count while we're having sex, does it?"

He chuckled. "If cock is your idea of a naughty word, then no. I like the way it sounds coming from your lips. Such a dirty Little girl. We'd better get you cleaned up, dirty girl."

He reached down to hold the condom in place and eased his semi-hard dick out of her, noticing her wince. "Sorry, Baby girl. You'll be sore for a few days. I promise it won't hurt like that the next time."

"Okay, Daddy."

He slid off the side of the bed, removed the condom, and wrapped it in a tissue before he swooped down and lifted her into his arms. After carrying her to the bathroom, he turned on the water and gently set her on her feet next to the shower.

She crossed her arms, shivering.

He wrapped her in his embrace. "Cold?"

She shook her head. "It feels strange being naked with someone. I didn't think about it while we were in your bed, but now that we're not, I feel self-conscious."

"Don't. There's no need. You're the sexiest woman I've ever set eyes on. Every inch of you."

"I'm a nerdy bookworm. You never even saw me with makeup, hair done, and a fancy dress until tonight."

"Oh, Baby girl, I saw you. I've always seen you. You don't need makeup or clothes or hairdos to impress me. You impress me without any of that." He tested the water and grabbed her hand. "Come."

She stepped in with him, holding his hand in a tight grip. Her gaze ran up and down his body. "You're like one of those statues of a god I've studied in art class."

He smiled at her. "You could pose naked on a chaise lounge and hundreds of people would gather to sketch you."

"Mmm. Should I do that?" she teased.

"Fuck no. Never." He faced her under the water, cupped her breasts, and kissed her. "All mine," he growled.

She shivered and bit her lip.

They stared at each other for a long time while the water ran over them. He knew they were thinking the same thing. Was she really his? For more than tonight? It was going to be complicated, but he vowed to make it work. Somehow.

Breaking the intense connection, he grabbed the shampoo, poured some in his palm and turned her around to wash her hair.

"God, that feels good. I'm going to smell like you. Do you think anyone will notice?"

"I don't know. Guess you better take another shower when you get home and not test that theory."

"Not a chance. I'm not going to bathe for days. I want your scent to linger on me."

He chuckled as he angled her head under the stream of water. "Close your eyes, Little Lyla."

"You make me feel so cherished," she whispered.

"That's the idea."

He put conditioner in next and let it sit while he grabbed the body soap. He took his time, lingering on her breasts until she was panting and arching toward him.

When he reached between her legs, he found her drenched and not just from the shower. She parted her feet for him and let him play with her folds until she grabbed his arm and started panting.

He stopped.

She whined. "Daddy. That's mean."

He laughed and tipped her head back again. "Your next orgasm will be even sweeter if I keep you on edge for a while."

After a groan, she grabbed the shampoo and jerked it from the rack. "My turn."

He took a step back and tipped his head forward so she could lather his hair. After he rinsed, she started on his body. She eventually found his cock and tormented him, turning the table and stroking his length until he thought he might come in her hand.

She released him. "You're right. That's kind of fun."

He groaned and grabbed her for a kiss. "Naughty, naughty girl."

She giggled, the sound going straight to his cock.

He turned off the water. "Come on. Let's get out of here. I need to taste you again."

Her smile was infectious as he dried her off and then himself. He tried to wring her hair out as much as possible before grabbing his comb. "Face the mirror, Baby girl."

She whimpered. "You're going to comb my hair? We could do that later. How about we go back to bed first?"

He gave her pink bottom a swat. "How about you obey Daddy and face the mirror?"

Her breath hitched as she grabbed the edge of the counter. Her fucking hot breasts hung in front of her, enticing him to suckle them again.

Soon. Drag this out. Make her beg.

Rock took his time working all the tangles out of her hair before setting the comb down and crowding her against the vanity. He trapped her with his hands on top of hers and kissed behind her ear. "Good girl," he whispered because he knew it would make her shiver.

"I need you, Daddy," she murmured.

He held her in place with one hand still covering hers while he used the other to cup a breast and toy with her nipple.

He would never forget her whimpers. The tone. The way her eyes fluttered. The way her mouth hung open.

When he smoothed his hand down her tummy and cupped her pussy, she rose onto her toes.

"Legs wider, Baby girl. Keep your feet flat."

She obeyed like a perfectly seasoned submissive. He'd never anticipated this reaction from her. This deep need to please him that matched his need to nurture her so completely.

Her head fell forward, the thick locks of her hair tumbling over her shoulders as she trembled for him.

He wouldn't penetrate her again tonight, but he would wring a few more orgasms out of her. Lips on her ear, he whispered, "Such a good girl for Daddy. So well behaved."

"Mmmm."

He played with her clit, driving her higher and higher, watching her every reaction and the way her tits were swinging in front of her. He loved the tight rosy tips. He loved her dainty, red-painted toes and her narrow waist and the flare of her hips.

He was suddenly the most possessive bastard on earth, and parting from her in a few hours was going to kill him. They had a few more days before he would leave for his internship, but there was very little chance they'd have the opportunity to spend this kind of time together again. Not without getting caught.

Her parents would lose their shit if they knew about this. It was a risk he was willing to take for this night of paradise, but he hoped for her sake they didn't get caught when he brought her home. He could take their wrath, but he didn't want her to suffer from their disappointment.

"Rock…"

"Do you need to come, Baby girl?" He flattened his thumb to her clit.

"Yes, Daddy," she murmured softly.

"Do it. Come on my hand while I watch you. I want to memorize the look on your face and the tremble of your sweet body."

Her breath hitched and she gripped the edge of the counter tighter as she arched her chest forward and let the waves of her release take over.

Rock wasn't exactly an old guy. He was only twenty himself. But having been raised around the MC he'd seen a lot of things. He'd never seen anything this special. This precious. This humbling.

When she was sated, he gathered her in his arms and lifted her to carry her back to bed.

As soon as they were settled on their sides, she snuggled into him. "I wish I could stay. I wish we were in our mid-twenties and I lived here and no one would judge us. I wish I could fall asleep in your arms and wake up at noon still pressed against you."

"I do too, Little Lyla." He stroked her cheek. God, he was already choking back the pain of parting from her. She wasn't like other women. She was an old soul. She knew her mind. She also knew her kink and wasn't denying it.

She was so perfect for him. If only she wasn't eighteen.

Suddenly, she pushed to sitting and gave him a shove so he fell onto his back. He would never forget her devious grin and the mischief in her gaze. "My turn."

He groaned and settled on his back. "Explore away, Little Lyla. I won't stop you."

As she turned her attention to his fully stiff cock, he set a hand on her back and stroked her soft skin. His focus shifted to her tits. They swayed as she settled onto her knees, grasped his erection, and lowered her lips to his dick.

Jesus. Fuck. He wasn't sure he would live through this.

She licked the tip, making him flinch before she lifted her gaze to stare at him through the curtain of her hair. "I have no idea what I'm doing."

He smoothed his palm up her back. "You do whatever feels right and nothing more. I don't need your lips on my cock to feel fulfilled, Baby girl. Kiss it. Lick it. Suck it if you want. Or none of that. Your choice."

He meant every word. He didn't need her to suck his cock if she didn't want to. He knew deep in his soul his job was to please her, and pleasing her was the only thing that mattered. It fueled him and filled his soul.

When his Little girl wrapped her lips around his cock and lowered her head down to suck him in deep, he groaned. He was still human.

She even hollowed her cheeks as she rose up and down. She wasted no time, and she didn't need any instructions.

Apparently, blowjobs were instinctive, or he'd given her enough advice to build her confidence.

Lyla was a dream. His own personal wet dream.

All too soon, he was on the edge, and he gripped her hair. "Baby girl, I'm going to come. If you don't want to swallow me, you need to pull off."

She lowered farther, sucking him deeper, doing something wicked with her tongue that had his eyes rolling back.

That was it. He couldn't hold back another second. He came harder than ever, emptying his seed against his girl's throat. There were no words for what she did to him. She unmanned him. She made him whole. She filled a part of him he'd known for a long time needed to be fulfilled.

He'd watched her for two years, and now she was in his bed, his cock in her mouth. He'd never felt this kind of peace and contentment as she lifted her face and smiled at him. "Did I do it right?"

CHAPTER
NINE

"R egrets?" Rock asked.

"God no. But when will I see you again?" she asked in barely a whisper. Her heart felt like it was going to break in two as she clutched her stilettos and the teddy bear in one hand.

It was five o'clock in the morning. She was leaning against the side of her house next to the door. She knew she could easily slip in and sneak up to her room without anyone knowing, mostly because she'd never once broken a rule or done something like this. She didn't even have a curfew because there had never been a need.

Rock crowded her. He had her pinned with his feet planted on either side of hers and his elbows next to her head against the brick. He kissed her behind her ear. "I don't know, Baby girl. I'll be around this weekend some with your brother. I'll find a way to pin you to a wall and steal a kiss," he teased.

She swallowed. "But I mean like after you leave for your internship and I go to school." Her knees were weak.

Most people would probably say she was far too young to feel the things she was feeling. They would also say Rock was.

But she knew better. She knew in her soul she would never in her life feel the things she'd experienced for the last six hours.

Rock set a hand on her chest between her breasts. The V of her dress allowed him to touch her bare skin. He set his forehead against hers and looked her in the eyes. "I can't predict the future, Little Lyla. But I do know you have to get your education and follow your dreams. I also know I will never leave this town. You will always be able to find me. We share a bond that will never be broken. One day our happily ever after will begin."

She swallowed back tears. "It already has, Daddy."

ROCK

I hope you enjoyed *Rock: The Prequel*. Are you ready for *Rock*? Jump ahead thirty-eight years and dive into their reunion.

CHAPTER
ONE

Lyla trembled as she pulled her car into the driveway of her childhood home. It was a surreal experience. She hadn't been here in almost forty years.

After taking a deep breath, she climbed out of the car and stared at the front of the house. She was surprised to see the same oak tree in the front yard. It was so large now that the entire yard was cast in shadow.

The house had probably been painted several times since she last saw it, but it was currently white—the same color it had been when she was growing up. The shrubbery was more recent, of course, and the railing on the porch had been replaced at some point.

Her phone buzzed in her pocket, so she pulled it out, knowing it would be her father calling. She smiled as she answered. "Hey, Dad."

"Did you make it okay, honey?"

"Yes. I just got here."

"Oh, good. I'm sorry to dump this on you, Lyla. It's asking a lot for you to take time out of your life to deal with selling the house. Thank you for taking care of it. Your mother and I appreciate it."

"It's no problem, Dad. I'll handle it. You just take care of Mom."

"Okay, honey. I'll talk to you later."

Lyla put her phone back in her jeans pocket and inhaled long and slow. She hadn't been here since the summer after she graduated from high school. Thirty-eight years. It seemed like a lifetime and yesterday all at once.

That June had been life-altering in many ways. She'd had her first kiss and lost her virginity on the same night. She'd fallen in love that night, too. She'd thought she was on top of the world. And then it had all fallen apart.

When her father's job transferred him to another state weeks after graduation, her parents decided to keep this house and use it as a rental. They'd done so for all these years. Her parents were in their eighties now, and her mother wasn't in good health. So they'd finally decided to sell it.

It was time to stop stalling and go inside. She wasn't expecting a disaster. The last tenants had been amazing folks who took good care of the place, but that didn't mean the house wouldn't need some work before it could be put on the market.

Instead of heading for the front of the house, Lyla aimed for the side entrance, the one she'd used most often. Her hands were shaking as she approached. She couldn't bring herself to reach for the handle.

Rooted to her spot, she stared at the wall next to the door and swallowed. She'd stood in that spot thirty-eight years ago, plastered to the wall, while Rock Monroe kissed the life out of her in the early-morning hours after a night of ecstasy.

Breathing heavily, she closed her eyes and leaned her forehead against the wall, picturing that night for the billionth time. She'd dreamed of it over and over. She'd never forgotten a detail, but now that she was here, it was so much more real.

She'd stood in this spot, her bare feet planted in the dirt, her prom dress askew, her hair a mess, her makeup long since smeared. She'd been deliciously sore from giving Rock her virginity. She'd also been filled with excitement from giving him her heart.

Rock had pinned her to the side of the house and kissed her over and over, one more last time after another. When he'd finally released her, he'd waited to make sure she made it inside safely, and then he'd sped off on his motorcycle.

Lyla had been eighteen years old. She'd lived two times longer since then. But she'd never forgotten that night, and she never would.

Was he living here in Shadowridge still today? She had no idea. She'd never inquired. Maybe she should look him up.

No. She couldn't.

He'd had a life since then. It would be too painful to find him married or perhaps even deceased. He would be fifty-eight now. Two years older than her.

She'd often wondered what had become of him, but she'd never allowed herself to search for him on social media. She needed to clean this house, get it up for sale, and let the past lie in the past.

CHAPTER
TWO

"Did you see that blue carpet on the walls?" Ink asked, chuckling.

Breaker laughed. "How could I miss it? It was godawful. I've never seen anything so hideous in my life."

Rock jerked his attention toward the two prospects who were sitting at the bar in the clubhouse, tipping back a few beers. He was standing behind the counter, looking for the box of snacks he'd stashed there a few days ago, hiding it from the Littles.

Grabbing the edge of the bar, he cleared his throat. "What did you say?" His voice squeaked.

Ink glanced at him. "Oh, man, you should have seen it. Breaker and I are doing a bit of work on a house in town. We're tasked with gutting a basement, and, man, does it need it. Some fool covered an entire wall with navy Berber carpet. Probably been there for decades. Whoever it was did a good job because it's a bitch to remove."

Rock's heart started racing, and it had nothing to do with the heart attack he'd had two years ago. He knew that basement. He knew it better than any other basement in town. He'd spent countless hours in that basement, studying with his friend, playing music, and hovering as close to his Little girl as possible.

The fool who'd stapled that carpet to the wall had been Jackson Sealock. Rock had been head over heels in love with his younger sister, Lyla, though he'd never once told Jackson that.

Breaker chuckled. "Some guy in the eighties probably put the carpet on the wall to help with the basement's acoustics. Guy probably played the drums too loud or something and drove his family nuts."

Rock was frozen, unable to move. Jackson had never played the drums, but he'd sure enjoyed his music, and he, indeed, had played it too loud. The carpet might have helped, though Rock had always thought it was a crazy idea.

"You okay, man?" Ink asked.

Rock finally managed to pry his fingers off the edge of the bar and nod.

Breaker laughed again. "What's even funnier is that the woman who's selling the house seems reluctant to have us take the carpet down. She hired us to do the job, but this morning, she paced in front of it, wringing her hands as though it was going to be physically painful for us to remove it."

Rock's breath hitched as his spine stiffened. "Woman?"

"Yep. Her parents own the place, and they've sent her to get it ready to sell."

Was it possible that Lyla and Jackson's parents had never sold the house? The idea was preposterous and farfetched. Wishful thinking. Rock needed to get his head out of his ass and straighten it on his shoulders. But a strange feeling crept up his neck, leaving goosebumps in its wake. "How old is this woman?"

Ink shrugged. "About your age, I'd guess."

Rock grabbed the edge of the bar again. He hated leaning toward the prospects, but he couldn't help himself. "Did you get her name?"

Ink glanced at Breaker, frowning. "Hmm. Do you remember? I think it started with an L. Lisa… Lyra…"

Rock stopped breathing. Holy fuck. "Lyla?" he managed to whisper as though just saying her name was somehow reverent.

Ink snapped his fingers. "That's it. Do you know her?"

Rock swallowed and shook his head. "I did. Years ago. Decades ago."

Breaker grinned. "Well, she's a looker, that one. For an old gal. Want me to tell her hello for you?"

Rock shook his head. "No. Please don't. I'll…" He had no idea what he might do. He needed time to wrap his head around this development.

He was stunned as he walked away, heading for his private apartment in the clubhouse. He owned a home a few miles from here, but he maintained this apartment for nights when he didn't feel like riding home.

As soon as Rock was alone, he shut the door and dropped onto his favorite recliner. He leaned back to stare blankly at the ceiling. Holy mother… Lyla was in town.

He'd never realized her family had kept the house. They'd been renting it out for nearly four decades?

Rock's heart was still beating fast. If a doctor saw him right now, he'd lose his mind.

Lyla… My God…

After all these years, she was here in Shadowridge. Would she look him up? Probably not. She was probably married with four kids and a dog. Grown kids. After all, Rock had been married and had two grown kids.

Kathy had died twenty years ago. Rock had loved her dearly, but she'd been gone longer than he'd known her by now. That seemed so strange. He'd never put himself back out there after Kathy had passed.

As far as Rock was concerned, he'd loved two women. The first had left town when he was twenty. The second had died too young. He'd never had any intention of loving another woman. It hurt deeply when they left him. It didn't matter the reason.

Rock had thought about Lyla often over the years. He'd wondered what had happened to her. Had she finished college? Gotten a teaching job? Had she married? Hell, he hadn't known if she'd even been alive until today.

She's here. In Shadowridge. Holy fuck.

One of the last things he'd told her was that he would always be here in this town if they ever lost touch. He'd never heard from her, and he'd never left town for any length of time. He'd lived here his entire life. She knew his name. It wouldn't be difficult to reach him.

Rock closed his eyes and let himself go back to that night nearly forty years ago. He would never forget the tears in her eyes when she returned home after her prom. She'd overheard her date and his buddies speaking crudely about fucking her.

Rock had wanted to strangle those little assholes in the moment, but Lyla had needed him to keep a level head. She'd needed a hug, and then she'd needed a lot more than a hug.

The next six hours had been the best in his twenty years of existence. He'd never forgotten a moment of it. The timing had been shit. He'd left town for a summer internship two days later, and she'd left the state for college two months later.

He'd thought they'd had something special that could withstand the test of time and distance, but he'd never heard from her again.

He'd been good friends with her older brother, Jackson, but they'd lost contact that summer, too. It hadn't helped that their parents had moved away, which meant Jackson and Lyla would have spent holidays and vacations wherever the Sealocks had moved.

With a groan, Rock rolled his head forward, set his elbows on his knees, and leaned his forehead against his palms. "Jesus…" he muttered. "She's here in Shadowridge." He couldn't wrap his head around that. He wanted to see her, if only from a distance. He wouldn't disrupt her if she was married, but what if she happened to be single like him?

Ink and Breaker hadn't mentioned anyone being with Lyla, but they hadn't said she was alone either. Would she be staying at the house? Doubtful. It probably wasn't furnished. It could be in serious disrepair. She'd obviously hired people to work on getting it ready to sell.

It was late. Rock pushed to standing. He'd considered staying here tonight but now changed his mind. He wanted to go home where he could be alone with his memories.

Even sliding his arms into his cut reminded him of the first time he'd met Lyla. She'd been sixteen. She should have been scared of him with his tattoos, torn jeans, black boots, and black leather Shadowridge Guardians MC jacket. She'd shown no signs of being leery of him, though. In fact, she'd met his gaze and stood toe-to-toe with him. She'd even asked about his Shadowridge Guardians logo.

Something about Lyla had drawn his attention and held it captive. She'd stolen his heart that day. He'd become good friends with her brother and hung around their home often from that day forward.

Rock had liked Jackson, but the real reason he'd cultivated that friendship was so he could see Lyla as often as possible. He didn't dare mention his attraction or instigate direct contact with her until she'd turned eighteen, but those two years had been long.

The one night he'd spent with her had been heaven and not nearly enough. The memories lingered. They'd lasted four decades. He still held a place in his heart for her.

As he was leaving his apartment in the compound, he ran into Remi in the hallway. His daughter cornered him with her hands on her hips. Kade, her husband and Daddy, stood behind her, smirking. This was becoming a regular occurrence.

Fending off the questions he knew would fly out of Remi's

mouth, he got a jump on her. "Yes, Remi, I ate dinner. No, I didn't have dessert. Yes, I ate the gross green things on my plate. Yes, I've taken my heart medicine. Yes, I walked today. No, I'm not in pain."

She gave him a slow smile and then wrapped her arms around him. "Okay, then. Are you going home for the night?"

"Yes." He kissed the top of her head before spinning her around and nudging her back to her Daddy. Kade would take care of her. He was a good man. "See you tomorrow."

It was a nice night outside. Great weather for a long evening ride. But Rock wasn't in the mood. He climbed on his bike, started it up, and pulled out of the compound.

He had no idea why he drove in the wrong direction and ended up on the street Lyla and Jackson had grown up on, but he slowed down as he went by the old house.

A light was on in the basement. He could see the illumination through the two small windows right at ground level. Was she in there? Surely not. It was getting late. She wouldn't be sitting in the empty basement. There were no other lights on in the house. There wouldn't be any furniture in there. She was probably at the motel on the edge of town. Maybe she forgot to turn the lights off.

There was a car in the driveway, but it was possible the neighbors used the spot since the house was vacant. That's what he would do instead of parking on the street.

For a minute, he considered driving toward the motel next, but that would be absurd. It wasn't as if he would know what car she drove or what room she would be staying in.

Granted, he did know the night manager for the motel, Sheila. He could go inside and ask her if Lyla was staying there. He had no idea what Lyla's last name might be. Surely it wasn't still Sealock. But that didn't matter. A description would be all Sheila would need to confirm if Lyla had secured a room.

Rock shook the idea from his head. *Don't be a fucking stalker, asshole*. It would be rude to ask Sheila to do something unethical. Besides, it was probably best that he not approach Lyla at all. She'd made a choice not to contact him after their one night together. He would respect her decision.

He drew in a deep breath as he aimed his bike toward his house on the outskirts of town. Anger bubbled up inside him, the same anger he'd felt that summer when she hadn't contacted him.

Rock has been hurt and confused. He'd given her a note with the number of the place he would be staying, the number of the office he'd be working for, and a number for the Shadowridge Guardians' clubhouse. She hadn't contacted him at any location, and once she'd gone off to college, he'd had no way to reach her.

He could have asked her brother, but he'd never let on to Jackson that he'd had any sort of relationship with Lyla at all, plus Jackson had vanished after that summer, too.

Rock pulled into his garage, shut off the engine, and climbed off his bike. His heart was heavy as he entered his dark house. He didn't even turn on any lights. He wasn't in the mood to see. After aiming straight for his bedroom, Rock removed his boots, brushed his teeth, and dropped onto the bed without pulling the covers back.

He stared at the ceiling, willing the memories to stop bombarding him. Lyla had never contacted him or returned to Shadowridge for a reason. Maybe she'd met someone that summer. Maybe she'd decided he wasn't good enough for her. Maybe her family had found out about the night she'd spent with Rock and demanded she sever contact.

He would never know why she'd vanished.

Unless he confronted her.

And that was a terrible idea.

Better to let sleeping dogs lie.

CHAPTER
THREE

L yla was imagining things. There was no other explanation for it. She'd been sitting in the basement of her childhood home for hours. The men who'd come to take a look at what needed to be done had left a long time ago. Why was she still here?

She'd gone to her car, grabbed her satchel, and had been sitting in the basement on the floor, leaning against the wall, sketching for hours. She could have sworn she'd heard a bike engine at some point, but she hadn't moved an inch. She'd paused, listened, and shuddered.

Surely she'd imagined it. Probably because she'd done nothing but think of Rock since she'd arrived here that morning. Was he still in town? Was he married? Did he still belong to the local MC? Had he ever thought of her again after that night they'd spent together?

Most likely, he didn't remember that night at all. It would be ridiculous to think he even remembered her name. Why would he? They'd had one night together, rolling in the sheets. That was it. He'd had countless other women. How many of them had been young and naïve? How many of them had been a virgin like she'd been?

She glanced down at her sketchpad, surprised to see that she'd been sketching images of Rock the way she remembered him. Five pages of him as a matter of fact.

Groaning at her idiocy, she shut the book and pushed to her feet. She looked around. This basement held so many memories. She couldn't believe the blue carpeting was still stapled to the wall. It was a dingy shade now, almost gray, but it was still there.

She turned around and stared where she'd been sitting the first time Rock had entered her line of sight. She'd been sketching a basket of fruit, and Jackson had ruined it by eating one of the apples.

She'd been sixteen. Most people would say she hadn't been old enough to know her mind, but she'd known a lot of things that day. She'd gotten close enough to Rock to inhale his masculine scent—the predominance of leather seeping into her memory.

He'd tucked her hair behind her ear, making her shiver then…and now. He'd smiled at her and looked her in the eyes. Even though he'd been rough, a biker, already a member of his MC at eighteen, she'd also known he was intelligent and wise.

That day had launched a crush she'd held for two years until the night he'd taken her to his apartment and shown her what it meant to be loved by a real man.

He'd ruined her for other men. She hadn't had sex again for many years because every time she'd gotten close enough to anyone to allow them to kiss her, she'd never felt the sparks she'd felt with Rock.

Had it all been an illusion? Maybe.

Yes, she'd eventually met Mike and gotten married. He'd been a math teacher at the high school where she'd taught art. He'd been kind to her and pursued her for two years before she'd finally given in and gone on a date with him. They'd become friends, and that friendship had grown into more.

Lyla had moved in with Mike the following year, and eventually, they'd gotten married. She'd been happy. Content. Things had been good until they hadn't been able to get pregnant.

Mike had wanted to see more doctors and try expensive infertility methods, but Lyla had never been dedicated enough to spend thousands of dollars on IVF. In the end, they'd separated and divorced. He'd moved to another state to start over.

Maybe everything that had gone wrong in their relationship had been her fault. It was possible she'd harbored feelings for another man and had never been able to fully invest in her marriage.

It didn't matter now. That was a lifetime ago.

Lyla took a deep breath and headed for the stairs. It was probably a horrible idea to have returned to Shadowridge to prepare her childhood home for sale. Feelings she preferred to leave deeply buried were rising to the surface and making her nervous.

There was no way she would seek him out. Nothing good could possibly come of it. He would be fifty-eight years old. If he was still in the MC, he was probably married. The best thing she could do would be to get this house ready for sale as fast as possible and get out of town. It would probably take a few weeks. She'd meant to stay and oversee everything, but maybe she should speed up her timetable for her own sanity.

After climbing into her rental car, she started the engine and pulled out of the driveway. Unable to resist, she drove toward the MC. The entrance looked the same as it had forty years ago. Maybe the fence had been replaced, but that was about it. There were a lot of bikes out front, but she didn't slow down. She simply drove by, her heart racing, wondering if Rock was in the compound. Her skin tingled at the thought that she might be yards away from him, a man she hadn't seen in decades. A man she's never forgotten.

Gripping the steering wheel, she headed toward the motel on the edge of town. She would be staying there until she was finished dealing with the house. If it weren't for the fact that her father really wanted her to make sure the house was in excellent condition so it could be sold at the proper market value, she'd lowball it, unload it to a house flipper tomorrow, and get the hell out of dodge.

But her father was all about making the most money on every transaction, and she had no legitimate excuse for not seeing this through. After all, she was a fifty-six-year-old retiree with nothing but time in front of her. She was in the prime of her life as far as she was concerned. After she got this house sold, she could take a long vacation somewhere, maybe hook up with a silver fox, and remind herself she was still alive.

Yep, that was an excellent idea. Why didn't it sound more appealing than it should?

She was dragging as she hauled herself into her motel room, dropped her satchel on the bed, and flopped down next to it. For a long time, she simply lay there, unable to stop thinking about Rock. Were the memories bombarding her just because she'd returned to town?

When she finally pulled herself up to get ready for bed, she shuffled into the bathroom, turned on the light, and stared at herself in the mirror. Who was she?

Lyla crossed her arms, suddenly feeling chilled. She didn't really know the woman staring back at her. She didn't think she looked as old as she was. She'd always taken care of herself. She was blessed with brown hair that hadn't turned gray yet. There were lines at the corners of her eyes, but most people had laugh lines.

She wasn't sure her lines were from laughing, though. Had she laughed enough in life? She'd done everything that was expected of her. She'd gotten a teaching degree like her parents had encouraged. They'd compromised between art and teaching when she'd agreed to pursue the combination.

She'd worked hard for thirty years. The students and other

faculty had loved her. She could have kept working, but she hadn't wanted to. Instead, she'd spent the last few years working on her own art, though she hadn't shared any of it with the world yet.

"You're boring," she told her reflection. "You've wasted your life away."

She knew it wouldn't look like that to an outsider. She had friends. She belonged to a gym. She had her book club. She had wine night with the other teachers her age. Bunco nights. Christmas parties. Vacations with friends or her parents.

"But have you lived?"

A tear came to her eye, and she quickly reached up to swipe it away. There was no need to cry or feel sorry for herself. She'd had a full life, and for fuck's sake, she was only fifty-six. She had many more years to enjoy herself.

"Doing what, Lyla?" she asked the mirror. "Huh? What are you going to do?" With a huge sigh, she went through her nightly routine of makeup removal, teeth brushing, flossing, and combing through her hair. She still kept it past her shoulders because she liked to be able to put it up in a ponytail.

Finally, she dropped into bed. When the sun came up, hopefully, she wouldn't feel so lost.

CHAPTER
FOUR

E ven though it had been nearly forty years since Lyla
had been to Shadowridge, she was surprised to find
that the local grocery store hadn't changed much. She
was pretty sure the butcher was the same man who'd been
there the last time she'd gone in.

She wanted to grab a cooler and pick up some lunch meat,
cheese, bread, chips, cookies, apples, and sodas. Things she
could keep in the house and hopefully feed the two guys who
were coming to do some construction work.

She was on edge for no good reason. Everything was fine.
She checked out and headed for her car. As she was loading
the trunk, the distinctive sound of a motorcycle rumbled as
one pulled into the parking lot.

Her heart raced as she took a deep breath. Hundreds of
people had motorcycles. The MC could be larger than ever by
now, but they weren't the only ones who owned bikes.

Lyla forced herself to ignore the single bike that was
parking near her.

Don't look up. Don't look up.

In her peripheral vision, she could see the black leather

jacket, the long legs covered in denim, and the black boots. Unable to resist, she lifted her head.

Her entire world shifted on its axis as she stared at a ghost. The box of sodas she'd bought slid from her hands to hit the concrete in front of her. She ignored it, unable to blink.

The man rushed forward. "Ma'am? Are you okay?" He bent to pick up the box and set it in her trunk before turning to her. His brow was furrowed.

She truly was looking at a ghost. It was Rock, but it wasn't. Obviously he would have aged. She hadn't gone back in time. She'd simply come home. "Rock?" It was ridiculous, but the question slipped out of her mouth before she could stop it.

His face changed in an instant. He smiled at her. "Do I look as old as that old fart?"

Her eyes went wide. Her jaw dropped open.

He chuckled. "Rock is my father. I'm Atlas."

Her heart was racing. Her entire body was shaking. Holy shit. She could see the differences now, but the two of them had many similarities, too. "Sorry," she murmured.

The man didn't move. "No reason to be sorry. Do you know my father?"

She drew in a breath. "I used to. A long time ago." This was inconvenient. Surely Atlas would tell his father he'd run into a woman who knew him. What difference did it make? Rock would never remember her. She could have been any woman from his past. Any girl from his high school years.

Atlas nodded toward the trunk. "I don't think any of the cans popped open, but I wouldn't open those for a while. You'll probably get sprayed in the face."

She tried to return his smile. "Thank you. Good advice. Sorry to be a bother."

"No bother at all. Should I tell my dad I ran into you?"

She waved a dismissive hand between them. "Goodness no. Don't even mention it. I was just startled, is all. I'm sure he wouldn't remember me."

Atlas stared at her for several more seconds. "And yet, you remember him well."

She swallowed.

He seemed to be assessing her. Finally, he broke the silence. "Well, it was nice meeting you. Have a nice day." Atlas slowly backed away before turning to walk into the store.

Lyla slumped against the trunk of the car, trying to catch her breath. She was a fit woman, but she'd felt like an exhausted ninety-year-old for the past twenty-four hours.

CHAPTER
FIVE

"Dad?"

Rock heard Atlas calling him as he passed his son's office in the clubhouse. He stopped and spun around to lean into the room, hand on the doorframe. "Sup?"

Atlas frowned. "You okay?"

"Yes. Why wouldn't I be?"

Atlas shrugged. "I don't know. You look more tired than usual. Are you sleeping okay? When do you next see your cardiologist?"

Rock stepped fully into the room, straightening his spine. He didn't need both his kids on his back about food and health. "I'm fine. Right as rain."

"Okay. You'll tell us if anything changes, right? Remi and I?"

"Of course." He waved a hand through the air. "Don't you worry."

As Rock turned to step back into the hallway, Atlas spoke again. "Oh, hey. I almost forgot to tell you. I ran into a woman at the grocery store this morning. I didn't get her name, but she thought I was you." Atlas chuckled. "It looked like she was seeing a ghost until I told her I was your son. She must have known you in high school. Did you have an old girl-friend you never told us about?"

Rock grabbed the doorframe again. This time, he thought he might collapse. His legs felt unsteady, and his chest was tight. The room started spinning.

He was aware of Atlas jumping up and rushing toward him, and then his son was helping him into an armchair in the office. "Shit. Fuck. Are you okay?"

Rock's hands shook as he brought them to his thighs. He couldn't speak yet.

"I'll get Doc."

Rock reached out and snagged his son's forearm, stopping him. "No need."

Atlas squatted in front of him. "Dad, you look like you're going to faint. I thought you would pass out on me. Something could be wrong with your heart."

Rock shook his head. "Nothing is wrong with my heart." He smirked. "Not from a ticking standpoint anyway."

Atlas's brows shot up. "Pardon?"

Rock gripped his son's arm tighter. He stared into his face. "How did she look?"

Atlas frowned. "Do you mean what did she look like? Brown hair, dark eyes. Mid-fifties. Though I probably would have said younger until I got it into my head that she knew you from a long time ago."

Rock shook his head. "I know what she looks like."

"Ohhh. Are you asking me if she was thin and sexy?" He laughed. "Dad, you old dog. Do you know who this woman is? I didn't even get her name."

"I know who she is."

Atlas's face sobered. He grabbed a chair, pulled it over, and sat knee-to-knee with his father. "Talk to me."

Rock sighed and ran a hand over his face. He stared past his son, uncertain he was ready for this discussion. If he was going to open this can of worms, he'd rather confront Lyla first. "Not yet."

"What's going on? How the hell did you know who I ran into at the grocery store before I even told you a thing about her?"

"Because Ink and Breaker saw her yesterday. I knew she was in town."

"Who is she?"

"A woman I...knew many years ago."

"Before Mom," Atlas said, not wording it as a question.

"Yes, way before your mom." Rock rose and stepped around his son. "I'm not ready to discuss this right now." He set a hand on Atlas's shoulder as he passed him. "Please don't say anything to Remi yet. Let me absorb this and deal with it in my own time."

Atlas tipped his head back to look up at Rock. "She's important to you."

Rock drew in a breath and nodded. "She was once, yes."

"Maybe you could ask around and find out where she is."

"I know where she is." Rock squeezed Atlas's shoulder and strode from the office.

It was obvious he was not going to be able to ignore the fact that Lyla was in town. It shook him to the core that she saw him in Atlas. Did she really remember him so well? Did it mean anything?

"Rock?"

As he wandered down the hall, heading for his apartment, Rock lifted his head. Feeling slumped and withdrawn, he forced himself to stand taller yet again as he faced King. "Yes?"

King frowned, much like Atlas had. The entire damn MC was always hyper-aware of Rock's health. He was surprised Doc hadn't come running down the hallway. The man had Spidey senses when it came to Rock's health. Hell, Doc had Spidey senses when it came to *everyone's* health.

"You look pale."

"I'm fine." How many people were going to ask him about his damn heart today? He needed to get out of here.

Luckily, he was saved from further discussion when King's Little girl, Ella, came running down the hallway and jumped into her Daddy's arms.

King braced himself, steadied her with a hand under her bottom, and scolded her, "What have I said about running in the compound?"

Ella pushed out her bottom lip and batted her eyes at him. "Sorry, Daddy."

Rock chuckled and took the opportunity to continue toward his apartment. He needed to think. He'd done very little *but* think since he'd first learned about Lyla being in town last night; he needed more time.

He needed to man up and drive to her house. Her presence was consuming him. He would never be able to get her out of his mind now. Especially since she'd spoken to Atlas.

Rock shut himself in his apartment and paced the small space. At least his kids couldn't harass him about not exercising.

He needed to see her more than he needed his next breath. Even if all he accomplished was a brief interaction, he felt compelled to do so. He had to know that she was okay. He had to know why she was in town. He had to know why she'd left.

Rock might not get all the answers. He might not ask all the questions. But he would at least see her, even if seeing her caused him to wake up in a cold sweat every night for the rest of his life. Letting her sell that house and drive away without getting closure wasn't an option.

CHAPTER
SIX

Lyla chewed on her bottom lip as she stared at the basement wall where the blue carpeting had been. Her brother had gone way overboard when he'd secured that crazy shit. He'd not only stapled it every few inches, but he'd also glued it. Ink and Breaker had needed to remove the drywall.

Lyla had taken lots of pictures. Feeling nostalgic, she'd considered calling her brother while the wall had come down. She hadn't wanted to talk to him, though. She couldn't get Rock out of her mind, and she didn't want to risk fielding any questions about the past from Jackson.

The nostalgia she felt was a bit overboard. She couldn't explain it. She hadn't been here since she was eighteen years old, and she'd never thought much about the house itself in all that time, but coming home was pulling everything to the surface.

It was late, getting dark out. She didn't want to sit on the basement floor until even later tonight, so she headed upstairs. As she packed everything up in her satchel, a knock sounded at the door.

Lyla turned to answer it, assuming it would be Ink or

Breaker. Maybe one of them forgot something when they finished up for the day. She opened the front door to find a man she didn't know standing on the porch.

He wore a battered gray ballcap with no logo. He shuffled his feet for a moment without lifting his face before suddenly darting into the house.

Lyla gasped as he grabbed her around the neck and shoved her backward.

Her adrenaline shot through the roof. Scared out of her mind, she screamed.

The man continued forward until he slammed her into the wall next to the entrance to the kitchen. He leaned into her, his face an inch from hers as pain shot through her from her head hitting the wall. The strike silenced her. She couldn't catch her breath to continue screaming.

"Where is it, bitch?" he hissed, spittle splattering against her face. His breath was disgusting. It wasn't from alcohol. It was from lack of hygiene. His teeth were gross. He probably hadn't brushed them in a long time. His eyes were bloodshot.

She tried to shove against him. "Help!"

He slapped her face with his free hand. "Shout again and I'll fucking slice your pretty face up until they can't identify your body, bitch. Where the fuck is it?"

She had no idea what he was talking about.

He grabbed her biceps with both hands and squeezed, pulling her forward and ramming her head into the wall over and over. His grip was tight.

What did he want? Was he going to rape her, or did he plan to rob her? Both?

Her teeth rattled as he continued to shake her. Her vision grew blurry. She feared she might pass out.

The sound of a motorcycle engine infiltrated her mind. Or maybe she was imagining it. She'd been hearing bike engines all day. She doubted many people on this residential street owned bikes, which meant she'd been conjuring the sound from her subconscious. After all, for the last two years she'd lived here, she'd heard a bike engine coming and going frequently. It had been Rock visiting Jackson every time. She wished to fuck he would show up now.

A loud sound, like a door slamming against the wall, made her flinch a moment before a deep voice rang out. "Get the fuck off her!"

The man instantly dropped her and dashed into the kitchen.

Lyla fell to the floor, landing on her hands and knees, shaking and gasping for breath.

New hands were on her a second later, making her cry out once more.

"Lyla, it's me. Rock. I've got you."

Rock?

She lifted her head to find the man she'd spent countless hours of her life thinking about squatting next to her. She blinked several times. Her mind was playing tricks on her.

Rock glanced toward the kitchen as another door slammed.

Lyla jumped. That would be her attacker getting away out the back. Another glance at Rock told her he was debating taking off after the guy. Part of her wanted him to catch the asshole, but she didn't want him to get hurt. She had no idea what shape he was in.

He turned his attention back to her and eased her onto her butt so she was leaning against the wall. "Are you hurt?"

She lifted a hand to rub the back of her head and winced as she tipped her head forward. "Is there any blood?"

Rock carefully guided her head forward more and gently moved her hair around. "No blood. You could have a concussion, though." He lifted her chin with a finger until she met his gaze.

His expression was fierce. It was the same expression he'd had that last night she'd seen him, the night he'd been waiting for her to come home from the prom and she'd told him how her date and his friends had spoken about her.

She wrapped her hand around his forearm. "I'm okay. Thank you for… Why are you here?"

"I wanted to see you. Good thing because apparently, my timing was impeccable." He pulled his phone out of his pocket.

"What are you doing?"

"Calling the police."

She nodded. Right. Of course. She started trembling, feeling cold for no reason. She vaguely heard him speaking to the dispatcher, and then he hung up.

"They'll be here in a few minutes." He stared at her some more, stroking her cheek. "You haven't changed."

She gave him a wan smile. "Your hair is gray."

He chuckled. "I'm old."

"You're only two years older than me."

"So I didn't age as well as you. Do you need to rub it in?" he teased.

She set her hands on the floor, wanting to stand.

Rock helped her to her feet.

Fuck, her head ached. She rubbed it, wincing when she reached her arms back to do so. They hurt, too.

"Let's get you some water," Rock said.

She nodded toward the kitchen. "There's a cooler."

He smirked. "I heard about the cooler."

She frowned as she followed him into the kitchen. "How?"

"Ink and Breaker. They're prospects for my MC. They're the reason I found out you were in town. I overheard them joking about the house with the blue carpet on the wall last night."

She winced as she rubbed her head.

"Tonight, they came back to the compound, pumping their chests about the smoking-hot older woman who'd fed them lunch and surprised them by treating them with respect even though they were covered with tattoos and wore MC jackets. They think you're the bomb." He grinned.

Damn, he looked fine. His hair was gray, but he was still fit and healthy as far as she could tell. His smile was the same. His eyes lit up every time he graced her with one.

Rock pulled a cold bottle of water from the cooler. He ran his hand down the outside of it to wipe away some of the excess water before opening the cap and handing it to her. "The electricity is on. Why didn't you put these in the fridge?"

"I had that cooler downstairs most of the day so the guys wouldn't have to come upstairs every time they needed a drink. Breaker carried it back up before they left."

It was surreal talking to him like this. Like no time had passed between them. He held her gaze for long seconds. "You haven't changed. You're still the thoughtful, kind Little Lyla I knew as a teenager."

She blushed and took a sip of the water to hide her thoughts. His voice did things to her. It hadn't changed either. His body might have aged, but his eyes were the same. His tone hadn't lost its depth. He was stroking her arm like he had decades ago. She felt like she was in a time warp.

Sirens filled the silence, and she set the water bottle on the counter to follow Rock into the front room. The door was still standing open. It had been the entire time. Rock had kicked it against the wall in his haste to get to her, but it had been ajar when Rock arrived to find her being assaulted.

Two officers entered the house. They greeted Rock with first names and handshakes, which made Lyla feel warm and relaxed.

The female turned to her. She held out a hand. "Officer Wright. Please, call me Susan, though."

Lyla took her hand. "Lyla."

The woman opened her phone and started typing. "Can I get your last name?"

"Sealock. Lyla Sealock."

Susan typed that in. "So, a man broke in and attacked you?"

Lyla shook her head. "No. He knocked. I answered the door. He pushed his way in and slammed me against the wall. I screamed a few times, but it was hard to continue with him shaking me so hard."

"Did he say what his intentions were?" Susan asked.

"No. He kept asking 'where is it?' as if I had something of his."

"And you have no idea what he was referring to?"

Lyla shook her head. "No."

"Have you ever seen him before?"

"No. I just got here yesterday."

Susan nodded. "Can you give me a description of the guy?"

"Five-eight, probably. Worn gray ballcap. Bad teeth. I think he was high. His eyes were bloodshot. He was strong but kind of skinny. There was a scar under his right eye, running toward his ear."

"Old or new scar?"

"Old," Lyla confirmed.

"What was he wearing?"

Lyla rubbed her temples, thinking, picturing him. "Dark hoodie, dirty jeans, work boots."

"I agree," Rock said from next to her. "He ran out through the kitchen when I got here, but I caught a look at him. I didn't see his face, but the clothing is what I witnessed."

Susan nodded.

Her partner, a man in his thirties, nodded toward the kitchen. "Mind if I take a look around?"

Lyla shook her head. "No problem. Go ahead. There isn't much left in the house."

"Sounds like the guy thinks you have something of his," Susan said as her partner disappeared.

"It makes no sense to me," Lyla informed her. "I've never seen him, and I'm not from town."

"How long has the house been vacant?"

"About a month."

"Could he have been squatting here?" Susan asked.

Lyla shrugged. "I suppose, but I haven't found evidence of that. There was no furniture or even a paper towel in this house when I arrived yesterday. Not even toilet paper. I bought supplies this morning."

"How long will you be in town?"

"I'm not sure. A few weeks. Just long enough to get the house on the market. It needs a bit of work." Lyla had been thinking about moving her timeline up a bit, mostly to avoid Rock. She still might do so, especially if some asshole was going to attack her again.

Susan shut her phone and pocketed it. "You should go to the emergency room."

Lyla shook her head. "I'll be fine. There's no broken skin." She winced as she rubbed several spots on the back of her head.

"You might have a concussion," Susan pointed out.

"I'll see that she gets medical attention," Rock stated.

The second officer returned to the front room. "I checked all the windows and doors. Nothing appears to be tampered with."

Lyla crossed her arms, shivering. "The sliding glass door off the kitchen wasn't locked when I arrived. I locked it and put the pole in place." She couldn't imagine how that mattered, but maybe it did.

Susan pulled her phone back out, presumably to note that. "Could be the guy was squatting here and you sealed his entrance. But you said there was no evidence, so that's unlikely. Maybe he mistook you for someone else."

Lyla hugged herself tighter. She had no answers. No one did.

The officers left her a card and said they would patrol the area to see if anyone fitting the description was lurking around. She gave them both her phone number and motel information. They would get in touch with her if they found anything out.

Suddenly, she was alone with Rock.

The first thing he said was, "You still have the same last name."

She faced him. "I changed it back after my divorce."

His brow furrowed. "So you're not married. Boyfriend?"

"No," she murmured, wondering about his wife. After all, he had kids. "You?"

"My wife passed away from cancer a long time ago. I never remarried."

She nodded slowly. So many questions ran through her head, but she couldn't decide where to start, and she needed some aspirin. Her head was killing her. She rubbed her temples again.

"Let's get you to the hospital."

"No. I'm fine. I don't want to spend the night in the emergency room. I just want to go to bed."

"Lyla, you could have a concussion."

"I don't."

He sighed. "Then, at least let me bring you to the compound so you can see Doc. We'll let him decide."

She scrunched up her face. She didn't feel like facing a bunch of people.

Rock licked his lips. "Yeah, you're right. I'll take you to my place. I'll have Doc meet us there."

His place…

"I have an apartment in the compound, but I also have a house on the edge of town. It's not much, but it's a place to sleep."

"I have a room at the motel," she said absently. There was no way she wanted to go there tonight. Out of the question.

She wouldn't feel safe with some guy hunting her for unknown reasons.

"We'll stop and get your things. You'll stay with me," he insisted.

She cracked a smile at his tone. "Still so bossy."

He lifted a brow. "Significantly *more* bossy than when I was twenty, Little Lyla."

She shuddered at the name he'd just used for the second time tonight. He'd called her that all the time when she was a teenager. "I'm not so little anymore," she pointed out.

He looked up and down her frame. "You're hardly larger, Little girl, but you also know that's not what I mean when I say Little," he challenged.

She shuddered again. She did know what he meant, but it had been decades since she'd even considered the idea of age play. Not since the night she'd spent with him. She'd never once met anyone in that lifestyle. She was aware of it. She'd researched the subject over the years. She'd read books about it —both fiction and nonfiction—but she hadn't practiced it.

Rock gathered up her satchel. "Is this all you have here at the house?"

"Yes."

"Where are your keys? I'll drive your car and have someone get my bike and drop it at my house."

She pulled the rental car keys out of her pocket and handed them to him. She wasn't going to argue. She certainly didn't feel like driving. Staying at his house, though… That was huge.

He pulled out his phone and appeared to send a few texts before ushering her out of the house. Like the gentleman she remembered, he opened the car door for her and helped her into the passenger seat. He also reached across to fasten her seat belt. "I'll be right back."

He shut her door and jogged over to his bike.

She watched in the mirror, wondering what he was doing.

Finally, he pulled something out of the bottom of the saddlebag and hurried back to the car. After he climbed in, he handed her a stuffed bear.

She slowly took it from him. Her heart rate picked up. He'd given her a bear the night of her prom when she'd been distressed.

He shrugged. "Maybe it's silly, but it's what we do in my club. When we encounter a damsel in distress, we give her a teddy bear. I'd say you're *definitely* a damsel in distress." He started the engine as if this was no big deal, but it meant the world to her.

She pulled the bear into her arms and held it tightly, lowering her face to inhale its scent of leather from being in the saddlebag for heaven only knew how long. "Thank you," she whispered.

"You're welcome, Little one."

She sucked back a breath. Little one. Was she Little?

As he started driving, he glanced at her and changed the subject. "Do you have kids?"

Apparently, they were going to get the big things answered immediately. "No. I...couldn't get pregnant. That was the primary reason for my divorce," she overshared. *No* would have been sufficient.

"I'm sorry."

She drew in a breath. "I think that came out wrong. I'm not sure I really *wanted* to have kids, so I wasn't willing to use heroic measures and thousands of dollars to have them. *That's* why we divorced."

"Ah."

"I met your son yesterday."

"I know. He told me." Rock grinned.

She looked at him, feeling confused. "I didn't give him my name."

"Yeah, but I already knew from Ink and Breaker that you were in town. So I figured."

"He looks like you. Do you have other kids?"

"A daughter, Remi. I'm proud of both of them. They're amazing."

"Are they in the MC?" She found herself wanting to know more and more about Rock. She was probably opening herself up for a world of hurt, but she couldn't resist the pull.

"Yes. Remi is married to one of our members, Kade. Atlas was gone for many years. He went to college out of state, became an accountant, and didn't come back until recently. We needed his help when our treasurer disappeared, leaving the MC's finances in shambles. Atlas reconnected with an old flame and stayed." Rock's smile grew. Apparently, he was very pleased with that development.

"That must be nice." She found herself smiling. She was happy for Rock.

"Yeah, except for them nagging me all the time," he groaned in a joking tone.

"What do they nag you about?"

Rock turned into the parking lot at the motel, parked next to the front desk, and turned to her. "I had a heart attack a few years back. I'm as good as new now, but they worry."

Lyla sucked in a breath and reached out to grab his hand. "I'm sorry to hear that. I'm glad you are well."

He set his other hand on top of hers, capturing it, squeezing it. "Thank you. Which room is yours?" He pointed toward the motel rooms.

"Oh, it's that one. Close. I'll just go grab a few things." She started to pull away, but he kept hold of her hand, stopping her.

She turned back to him to find him frowning again. "You'll wait for me. Let me talk to Sheila and tell her you're checking out. Then I'll help you pack everything up."

Lyla's breath hitched. "I can't impose on you for more than one night."

He narrowed his gaze. "You will never be imposing on me,

Little Lyla. I know it's been a few years since we last saw each other, and we're feeling awkward, but I wouldn't feel right leaving you alone in a motel, no matter who you were, after what happened tonight. You'll stay with me."

She swallowed and nodded, unable to deny him. She was scared out of her mind and freaking the fuck out inside, but she couldn't tell him no. It was difficult to keep her mouth closed and not point out that "a few years" was a gross understatement.

CHAPTER
SEVEN

R ock's head was spinning. He couldn't believe this was happening. An hour ago, his world had shifted on its axis, and now he was living a different life. One with Lyla in it. One with Lyla in his home.

He'd never imagined he would spend more than a few minutes with her when he headed over to her house earlier. Hell, he hadn't been sure if she would still be there or if he would even stop and confront her at all.

He'd about lost his head when he saw the front door open and then heard her distressed voice. He'd never moved so fast in his life. He was still kicking himself for not taking off after her assailant who'd run out the back, but he'd been more worried about Lyla than catching the guy. He hadn't been sure how injured she was.

He jogged around her rental car to help her out of the seat and took her hand as he led her into the main office. Possessive much? Yes.

Sheila was behind the desk when they stepped inside. She looked up, smiled, and then made a small gasping sound, eyes wide. "Oh, hi, Rock. I didn't know you knew Lyla."

"Yep. We knew each other in high school." He was well

aware it was over-the-top to be touching her so possessively. Way over-the-top *and* presumptuous, but he couldn't help himself. And he had no interest in stopping, especially since she wasn't trying to pull away.

Sheila reined in her surprise and pasted on a more professional expression. "What can I do for you?"

"Lyla is going to check out and stay with me. Someone attacked her in her home this evening, and he got away. Until the police catch him, I don't think it's safe for her to stay at the motel alone."

Sheila set a hand over her heart. She shifted her attention to Lyla. "Oh my God. That's awful. I'm so sorry."

Lyla gave her a small smile. "I'll be okay. Thank you."

Sheila clicked on her computer. "I'll get you checked out right now. There will be no charge for tonight."

"You don't have to do that," Lyla argued. "I can pay for the week that I booked."

Sheila shook her head. "Not necessary. Don't even worry about it. It's all taken care of." She gave a final dramatic click on the keyboard and turned back to face them. "I hope they catch him."

"They will," Rock growled. They most certainly would. As soon as the MC found out what had happened, every member of his club would be on the lookout. "Thank you, Sheila."

He led Lyla out the door and over to her room. When she pulled her keycard from her pocket, he took it from her. He didn't think anyone was lurking around the area, but he wanted to check in the room before he let her enter.

"Stay here," he ordered as he opened the door.

Lyla nodded. At least she wasn't arguing with him.

He stepped inside, leaving her holding the door. It was just one room and a bathroom, so it took him seconds to decide that no one had broken in, nor were they still there. "Okay."

Lyla entered and let the door shut. She looked nervous. He

couldn't blame her. Her face was pinched, too. "Does your head hurt, Little one?"

She nodded.

"Doc will meet us at my place and look you over. Then we'll get you some pain meds and you can sleep." He closed the distance between them and lifted her face. Holding her gaze, he continued, "I would apologize for airing your business to Sheila, but the truth is the entire town will know about the attack before morning. Telling Sheila won't stop that."

Lyla nodded. "I know. I used to live here." She smiled.

"Things haven't changed," he confirmed. "Shadowridge is still a small town."

Lyla sighed. "Of course."

"I will apologize preemptively for my dominance. We're not the same people we were back then. I have no business dominating you the way I am, but it's in my nature. It's who we were together. I don't know another way to be—not with you, and not with anyone. I do want you to know that I haven't dated or been in a relationship for a very long time, so this side of me is rusty."

She bit her lip. Was she fighting a grin?

He narrowed his gaze. "Don't get me wrong. My MC is filled with Daddies and Little girls. I dominate every one of them, but I'm not *their* Daddy, so it's not the same."

"You're not *my* Daddy, either," she murmured.

He swallowed. Wasn't he, though? He had been the last time he saw her. He'd been her Dom in every way. She'd submitted to him like a precious angel. He'd subtly dominated her for two years before that night they'd spent together, and it had easily come back as soon as they'd been alone.

In many ways, it felt like time had stood still, like nothing had changed since the last time he'd seen her. They were older and wiser, with life experiences they would need to share, but the dynamic between them had not changed. It was snapping back into place as if time had not passed.

She stared at him with wide eyes, challenging him with those last words she'd spoken.

Rock pulled her into his arms, hugged her close, and slid one hand into her hair. God, she felt good. His heart may have misbehaved a few years back, but it was ticking fine now. He hadn't felt this alive in years.

Her hair was exactly as he remembered. Soft and thick. It was almost the same length, and it hadn't turned gray. Sure, she was older. There were lines on her face. She was a few pounds heavier, but she'd been so young and had not finished filling out at eighteen. She was exactly perfect. And she felt so fucking good in his arms.

He couldn't manage to let her go, and he loved the way she slowly wrapped her arms around his middle and held him, too. She even sighed as though relaxing into him.

He had questions. Millions of them. Why had she left and never looked back? He'd spent all these years thinking she hadn't thought he was good enough for her or that someone else had convinced her he wasn't. He hadn't had any other explanation for her disappearance without a word.

They would get to that. They would discuss everything. But, for now, he needed to pack her up and get her home.

Home.

His home.

Suddenly, the thought of having her in it made him finally feel more relaxed. He'd been off for the past few years, pacing at night, feeling out of body and not at rest. Not at peace. He'd thought a lot about Lyla, more so since his heart attack than before.

The health scare had made him face his mortality, and he hadn't liked it. Holding Lyla made him feel alive again.

It was far too soon to predict what might happen between them, but he was hopeful. Perhaps foolishly so.

He didn't address her comment. No, he was not her Daddy, but he'd give just about anything to be so. They didn't need to talk about it. He would show her, win her over. He could feel it in his bones.

It would destroy him if she hadn't felt like he was good enough for her back then, but he would find a way to make peace with it. All that mattered was how she felt now. If she'd been judgmental or allowed others to influence her at eighteen, that didn't mean she would feel that way now.

It had never added up because Lyla had never once given him a single indication that she'd cared about him belonging to an MC or his tattoos or his cut. In fact, if anything, she'd always seemed in awe of him. She'd looked at him longingly as though he'd hung the moon. He'd had the impression she'd felt unworthy, as if *she* were the one who hadn't measured up instead of him.

He'd never been able to make sense of her disappearance, and he had no more answers now than he'd had then. Time. They needed to get to know each other all over again.

He reluctantly tipped her head back and met her gaze, staring into her eyes for a long time. They hadn't turned the lights on yet. There was nothing more than the streetlights coming in from the parking lot. It was enough, though.

She wasn't pulling away from him, and that hit him hard in the feels.

He set his forehead against hers. "Let's get you packed up." His voice was gravelly.

"Okay," she murmured.

Rock reluctantly released her and took a step back, looking around.

Turning toward the door, she flipped on the overhead light before closing the blinds. Next, she grabbed her suitcase from the corner, set it on the bed, and opened it.

"Can I help in any way?" He felt ridiculous just watching her, but he didn't have the right to start rummaging through her things or touching her lingerie. Yet.

If she were his… Fuck, she would not be packing at all. He

would sit her down and do it for her. But that was going too far tonight. He needed to back up a step and let her fill her own suitcase.

She nodded in the direction of the bathroom. "You could grab my toiletries while I pack the suitcase." She stepped toward the drawers.

"Got it." He turned toward the bathroom, found her makeup bag on the shelf under the sink, and filled it with everything on the counter.

When he returned to the bedroom, she was stuffing what he assumed was the last of her things into the large suitcase. He set a hand on the bed to lean over and hand her the case.

His palm landed on something lumpy in the bed and he set her toiletry bag on the suitcase and rose to pull the sheets back.

His breath hitched, and he staggered backward.

At the same time, her breath hitched, too, and she froze.

Rock leaned against the wall, staring at her, rubbing his mouth with his hand.

"I…" She closed her mouth and pursed her lips.

They stood there staring at each other for long seconds. His heart was beating so fast it threatened to explode out of his chest. He swallowed hard, fighting the emotional overload. He was a dominant man. He'd always been this way. He could be firm and bossy. He could make the Little girls in his MC tremble with fear when he threatened to tell their Daddies about their naughty behavior.

But right now, he was feeling too emotional to utter a single word.

It was Lyla who finally broke the standoff by reaching down to pick up the teddy bear from the bed. Not the one he'd given her ten minutes ago. The one he'd given her *forty years* ago.

She brought the bear to her chest and held him tight. "I didn't always sleep with him," she whispered as though he needed an explanation. "I just… Recently… Especially when I knew I was coming here. Things… They came to the surface. Feelings. I…"

He shoved off the wall, rounded the bed, and pulled her into his arms again. This was fucking huge. She couldn't explain it away. Any thought he'd ever had that she maybe didn't remember him fled the room. She'd been sleeping with the bear he'd given her forty fucking years ago last night, for fuck's sake.

He cupped the back of her head and held her gaze. The bear was smashed between them where she clutched it against her. He gave her plenty of time to turn away, but she didn't. And he lowered his lips to hers slowly.

He could have devoured her, but instead, he kissed her sweetly, just enough to remind her of the chemistry between them. He wouldn't take more. She was injured. He needed to get her home, let Doc look her over, and feed her. He needed to tuck her into bed with some painkillers.

He nibbled against her lips, loving the way she whimpered and leaned into him. He spread his hands on her back and enjoyed the feel of her. Peace swept over him. A peace he hadn't known in years.

Home.

His Little girl was home. He knew in his heart he would never let her go. Did she realize that? Whatever the fuck had happened over the past forty years would be water under the bridge.

He couldn't possibly watch her drive away from him. Not a chance.

CHAPTER
EIGHT

Lyla sat silently on the drive to Rock's house. She didn't know what to say. She was a ball of nerves. Things were happening so fast. He'd kissed her.

Could she blame him? After all, what did she expect would happen when he discovered Rock the Bear on her bed? She'd forgotten about the stuffie until he'd pulled the covers back, and there hadn't been a thing she could possibly have said to weasel her way out of that situation.

The teddy bear spoke volumes. There were no words.

She wasn't surprised to discover that Rock's house was at the end of a narrow street with only a few homes on it. The space between the houses was large. He probably owned a few acres. The porch light was on, and she could see that the home was like a log cabin with a natural wood exterior.

He parked and rounded the car to let her out. She didn't even bother to open the door herself. It seemed important to him to help her. Plus, she liked the way he Daddied her. She hadn't experienced this level of dominance since the last time she'd seen him.

After that night, she'd stuffed her submissive side deep down and ignored it, never to pull it out again. She'd moved on. Gone to college. Gotten a teaching job. Eventually married Mike. She'd never mentioned a word to her husband about craving any sort of D/s relationship. He hadn't given her any indication he would be receptive to the idea.

Here she was, a fifty-six-year-old woman clutching two teddy bears in her arms and staring up into the eyes of a man she'd loved dearly as a teenager.

He helped her out of the car and led her to the small porch. "It's not a big house, but it's home."

"Did you raise your kids here?" she asked. The question she really wanted to know was, had he lived here with his wife?

"No. I've only owned this for about five years. I've only lived here on my own." He opened the door, flipped on the lights, and nodded inside. "Go on in. Make yourself at home. I'll grab your things."

She turned and watched as he jogged back toward her car. The sound of a bike engine made her lift her gaze to see a single headlight coming toward them. That would be Doc.

She wasn't thrilled by the idea of someone examining her. She didn't think it was necessary. But she would do it. For Rock. To ease his mind.

Rock brought her things up to the house and set them just inside the door as the tall man climbed off the bike.

When the man joined them on the porch, she could see him better. Mid to late thirties. Brown hair. Blue eyes. A friendly, warm smile. He held out a hand. "Lyla, right?"

"Yes." She shook his hand.

"I'm Doc."

She giggled. "That's your name?"

He winked. "That's what all the Little girls call me. The MC members, too."

"Okay." She wouldn't ask his real name.

"Let's go inside," Rock said, setting a hand on Lyla's waist to guide her into the house.

Doc followed and shut the door. His expression switched to one of concern. "I understand you were attacked earlier?"

"Yeah. I don't think I'm severely injured or anything. My head hurts."

Rock growled. "He slammed her head against the wall repeatedly and shook her hard."

"Better safe than sorry, Little one. I'll check you out and then let you get some sleep, okay?"

Why did he assume she was Little? Maybe he simply called every woman Little one. Rock had indicated most of the members of the MC were Daddy Doms, so maybe most of their wives and girlfriends were Little.

"Let's go into the bedroom," Rock said. He set a hand on the small of her back and guided her toward the two doors on one side of the room.

She looked around, realizing this cabin was very small. She was in a great room, with one-half being the kitchen area and the other half being the living room. As she stepped toward the two doors, she noticed one was a bathroom, and the other was a bedroom. That was it.

It was cozy. Rock was obviously a minimalist. Everything was inviting, though. The colors were all browns, dark oranges, and reds. The furniture was rustic, perhaps custom-made. The floor was hardwood. The walls were wood paneled.

It wasn't modern, but she loved it. She loved the warm feeling.

Rock turned on the lights as she entered the bedroom, and she found it to follow the same basic theme. He had a queen bed, a matching dresser, a small desk, and two nightstands. All of them also looked like a custom design.

"Have a seat, Little one," Rock said softly, pointing toward the bed.

The quilt was also brown and orange and red, matching the pillows on the couch in the living room. As she lowered to sit on the edge, she realized she was still clutching the two teddy bears. She'd shifted them into one arm absentmindedly when she'd reached to shake Doc's hand. She quickly turned to set them on the pillow, her face heating at the fact that Doc had seen this side of her. No wonder he'd called her Little one.

Doc grabbed the chair from the desk and pulled it over to sit in front of her. He nodded toward the bears. "One of those is very loved. I bet Rock gave you the other tonight."

Rock came to her side and set a hand on her shoulder. "Rock gave her the older one thirty-eight years ago," he declared, sounding like the Dom he was.

Doc's brows lifted. "Is that so?" He shifted his attention back to Lyla. This was when she noticed he was holding a medical bag, which he set on the bed next to her. He opened it and pulled out a small light. "This will be bright, but I want to look at your pupils, Little one."

She tipped her head back and held her breath while he pulled her eyelid back and looked into her eye. He switched to the other one and then back and forth another time. "Pupils look good."

She breathed out a sigh of relief. The last thing she wanted was for him to decide she had a concussion and order her to go to the hospital. She was certain the pain was external.

Doc stood. "Can you tip your head down for me so I can see the back?"

She lowered her head toward her lap and winced as he prodded around the area of the injury.

"Tender?"

"Yes."

"The skin isn't broken. There's some swelling, but it's not bad. If it hurts, you can put ice on it for a while, but I suspect what you'd really like is some Tylenol, some warm soup, and sleep."

"Yes." *Please*. Her energy was waning.

Rock grunted. "The fucker grabbed her arms, too. He was holding her by the biceps and shaking her."

Lyla looked at Rock. "It's fine, Rock."

He frowned.

Doc touched her shoulder. "Let's take your shirt off so I can make sure. Is that okay?"

She drew in a slow breath. Of course it was okay. He was a doctor. She had a bra on. It wasn't like she would be naked. But she was nervous anyway. She glanced at Rock. This was awkward.

He gently cupped her chin and tipped her head back farther. "Little girl, I've seen every inch of your naked body. I'm not leaving the room. Let the doctor check your arms."

There was so much to read in his words and tone. Dominance. Hope. Promise. Reverence.

"Okay," she whispered, swallowing her nerves.

Rock reached for the hem of her long-sleeved shirt and lifted it over her head.

As the air in the room hit her naked skin, she shivered. She was wearing a simple white bra because that was all she owned. It wasn't like anyone ever saw her lingerie, and she certainly hadn't expected to be in a position like this when she'd arrived in town.

Goosebumps rose on her skin.

Rock brushed her hair back from her face and surprised her by leaning over to kiss her forehead. "Good girl."

Her breath hitched. He'd said that to her all those years ago, and she reacted the same to the praise today as she had back then.

Doc lifted one of her arms and gently examined it. "You're going to have some dark bruising here in about a day, but it will heal."

When she looked at Rock, she found his teeth gritted. He was furious. She kind of liked that he was so angry on her behalf.

Doc took his time examining the other arm next. "I can prescribe some stronger pain meds if you find you need them, but I bet Tylenol will be sufficient." He turned toward Rock. "You can give her two every four hours during the night. Her head is going to hurt, but she's not concussed. You don't need to wake her up or anything. Just watch to be sure she's not in pain."

Doc smiled as he looked back at her. "I don't like Little girls to be hurting."

She bit her lip. He assumed she was Little. Why wouldn't he? Maybe she was.

He stood and gathered his bag. "Call me if anything changes or she's in too much pain."

"I will. Thank you, Doc." Rock lifted Lyla's chin again. "I'm going to see him out. Don't move." He raised his brows.

She licked her lips and said nothing.

He leaned in closer. "Lyla…"

Did he need her to answer him? "Okay. I won't move." She tried not to sound sassy, but it came out that way anyway.

Rock gave her a slow smirk and then a warning chuckle.

As he left the room with Doc, she blew out a long breath and shivered from head to toe. Holy shit. Rock was so intense. And even though she was in pain and her head was now pounding, her body was alive like it hadn't been in years. Her pussy was soaked, leaking onto her panties. Her nipples were hard points, and it wasn't from the chill in the air.

The room was spinning. Not because she was dizzy but because her life was upside down.

She grabbed her shirt and held it up against her chest as a tiny barrier. There was no way she could put it back on. Lifting her arms hurt. Now that she was sitting still, everything ached more than it had for the past two hours. Her arms were throbbing.

Rock came back into the room less than a minute later. He headed for the dresser first, opened a drawer, and pulled out a T-shirt.

He came to her side. "Are you cold, Lyla?"

"No," she murmured.

"Can I help you put a T-shirt on and get out of your jeans?"

She tipped her head back. "Rock..." She didn't even know what she wanted to say. So many things. *I'm scared. I don't know you. I know you too well. Stop being nice. Please hold me. What's happening here?* The list was long.

He squatted down so he was at eye level with her. "I'm going to take your bra off and put this shirt on you, Little one. Okay?"

She drew in a deep breath.

"Baby girl, I've seen you naked before," he pointed out a second time.

Baby girl... He was going *there* now? She had to fight back tears. He'd called her that several times the one night they spent together. It had felt so nice then, and it felt nice now, too.

"That was forty years ago, Rock. I've changed a bit." Inside and out.

"Are those still your boobs?" he teased.

She rolled her eyes. "If they were storebought, they would not sag like they do."

He chuckled. "I think you look exactly perfect, and I don't give a shit if your boobs aren't as far north as they used to be. None of my parts are, either."

She didn't have the energy to reach back and unfasten her bra. Plus, her arms would scream if she twisted them that way, so she relented. "Fine."

After standing, he was quick about leaning over to undo her bra, and then he pulled the T-shirt over her head without making a big deal or looking directly at her chest. "Can you lift your arms for me, Little one?"

She released the shirt and the bra and let them fall to her lap before lifting her arms just high enough for him to get her hands through the sleeves.

"There," he declared. He squatted in front of her again and

removed her shoes and socks. "You want me to take your jeans off?"

"I can do it." She didn't need his hands that close to her pussy. She would die of mortification.

"Okay. When did you last eat?"

"Lunch." She'd intended to pick up something on her way to the motel.

"I'm not a great cook, but I'm amazing with a can opener. How about chicken noodle soup and crackers?"

She smiled. "That sounds perfect. Thank you."

"I'll put your toiletry bag in the bathroom. You go potty and get under the covers. I'll bring you some soup in bed."

Her heart was racing again. He was Daddying her. Hard. It frightened her and warmed her heart at the same time. "Okay."

He kissed her forehead and left her alone in the bedroom.

She looked around. There was only one bed in this house. It wasn't even a king. The couch hadn't looked big enough for Rock to sleep on, and besides, she would never kick the man out of his own bed. She was an adult. She could share his bed without mauling him in her sleep. Couldn't she?

After removing her jeans, she padded quietly to the bathroom, glancing at Rock's fantastic backside where he was standing at the stove. Damn, the man was just as smoking hot as he had been when he'd been twenty. Actually, maybe he was hotter. She was loving the silver-fox thing.

She found her toiletry bag on the vanity, opened it, and went to work removing her makeup, brushing her teeth, and using the toilet. When she returned to the bedroom, he was setting a steaming bowl on the nightstand.

He'd pulled the covers back and patted the bed. "Climb in, Little one."

"I'm not sure age play is going to work for me at this stage in my life," she pointed out, concerned about his expectations.

He gasped dramatically as he helped her get situated

against the headboard with several pillows behind her. He pulled the covers up over her legs. "No one is too old for age play or any other kink, Little Lyla. Blasphemy."

She couldn't keep from rolling her eyes.

He sat on the edge next to her and set a hand on her thigh over the covers. "I can't believe you're here."

"It's certainly strange. I can't believe I'm nearly naked in your bed, wearing your T-shirt."

He gave her a slow, sexy smile. "I want you here. I can't explain how instantly I knew I wanted you here. I know we have a lot to talk about, but, Lyla, I want you here."

He'd said it three times. Apparently, he meant it. She couldn't respond because she was choked up.

Rock lifted her palm and set two Tylenol pills in it from the bottle on the nightstand. He handed her a cup of clear liquid next. Not just any cup but one with a spill-proof lid. It wasn't entirely babyish. Adults used spill-proof lids sometimes, but she suspected it meant something different to him.

She took a long drink, feeling better already. She was dehydrated.

He held up the bowl of soup next. "Do you want me to feed you, Little Lyla?"

She shook her head. She wasn't ready for that. It was too intimate. Too...Daddyish. "I'll do it." She took the bowl from him, held it under her chin with one hand, and spooned some into her mouth with the other.

He watched her intently, stroking her leg as she ate.

It was hard to ignore him, but she was hungry, so she did her best to eat the entire bowl without panicking over the madness that she found herself in.

"Do you want more, Baby girl?"

She shook her head as she handed him the bowl. "No, thank you. I'm good now."

He set it aside, stood, and helped her slide under the covers before fluffing the pillow behind her head. He handed her the two bears.

Lyla rolled onto her side, alleviating the pressure against the back of her head.

"Are you comfortable?"

"Yes, thank you. So tired." Her voice was growing faint.

He bent and kissed her temple. "I'll be on the couch if you need me."

She reached out and grabbed his hand. "Don't sleep in the living room. This is your bed. We're grown adults. I think we can share a bed and keep our pants on."

He smirked. "Baby girl, you already don't have your pants on."

She rolled her eyes again. "Turn off the lights and get in bed, Rock."

He chuckled. "Bossy."

"When it's necessary, yes."

He kissed her temple again. "Sleep, Little Lyla."

She closed her eyes, hugged the two bears against her chest, and took a deep breath. She'd never slept with Rock before. The night they'd spent together hadn't involved any sleeping. This was new.

She was so very tired, though, and vaguely aware of him moving around the house. She kept expecting the bed to dip next to her, but she drifted off before it happened.

CHAPTER
NINE

R ock did his best not to jostle the mattress much when he joined Lyla. He slid under the covers as carefully as possible, wearing loose cotton shorts and boxer briefs. Neither was keeping him from having a constant hard-on.

He'd turned all the lights off, but his nightlight glowed next to the bedroom door. Remi had put it there after his heart attack because she'd been worried about him falling in the night. He'd left it ever since. He hardly noticed it, but it was providing him enough light to stare at his Little girl now.

His Little girl?

Shit. She was not his. She'd come to Shadowridge to sell her parents' house. She hadn't even sought him out. He'd come to her. Would she have done so eventually? He wasn't sure.

She was here now. In his bed. In his shirt. Hugging the two stuffies he'd given her. It made his chest tight to realize she'd kept that bear for all these years. It brought him to his knees. And now she was lying on her side, curled up around the two bears as though they were tethering her to Earth.

Fuck, she was precious. She didn't look anywhere near as

old as she was. In fact, he felt ancient next to her. Her hair was still brown, and he couldn't resist the urge to reach out and brush it away from her temple.

She was facing him, which gave him the ability to stare at her, but it also meant he couldn't wrap himself around her and spoon her. He'd dreamed of spooning Lyla most of his life. He'd often regretted that they'd never actually slept together—eyes closed—in his bed. They'd made good use of his bed, but they'd spent every second talking, teasing, fucking, learning each other's bodies. He hadn't had the chance to stare at her in her sleep or hold her against his chest.

Her lips were parted, and her face was smoothed out. Now that the painkillers had kicked in, she no longer had stress lines between her brows.

He smiled as he remembered the first time he'd seen her. She'd been awkward and nervous; he'd known it was because she'd also found herself attracted to him. She'd been the most adorable person he'd ever set eyes on. Nothing detracted from his instant attraction—not her braces, her glasses, or her gangly, not-quite-adult body.

Rock had kept his hands and his thoughts to himself for two years. He hadn't intended to claim her the way he had on her prom night, either. He'd waited for her because he'd wanted to know how her evening had gone, but taking her home with him and deflowering her hadn't been on his radar.

He'd never regretted a moment of that night, though he suspected she had. Why else would she have disappeared, never to return?

Eventually, he forced himself to relax against the pillow, his gaze still on her, mere inches separating their faces.

Lyla is in my bed. Please, God. Please let this be permanent. I never want to spend another night without her for the rest of my life.

There were so many unknowns. So much to discuss. They had a forty-year hole to fill, but his heart told him he would do anything to work it out and make her his for good.

Should he have tried harder to find her back then? Maybe. The ball had been in her court because she'd had his contact information. He'd had nothing. He'd known which university she attended, but it was on the other side of the country, so what could he have done? Driven there and stood around until she happened to walk by him?

He'd lost contact with her brother at the same time. It wasn't like they'd had email and cell phones. He hadn't even known where her parents had moved.

Rock had been the constant. After his internship, he'd returned to Shadowridge, taken a job in town, and never left. Yes, he'd lived. He'd met and married Kathy. He'd had two amazing kids with her and loved her to pieces. Losing her to cancer had been rough. She'd been his Little and his partner. She'd now been gone for twenty years. So long.

Rock had never remarried or even dated. He'd hooked up with women from time to time, but nothing serious. Oddly, in recent years, he'd found himself thinking about Lyla more and more. Foreshadowing?

And now she was here.

Forcing himself to close his eyes, he took deep breaths. Part of him feared he would wake up and find out this entire evening had been a dream. He wouldn't wish harm on Lyla for any reason, of course, but the fact that she'd been attacked was the reason she was in his home.

He reached out with his hand and set it on one of the bears. He didn't want to touch her and risk waking her, but he wanted to feel connected to her through the bear. If she moved, he would know.

And he did. Some time later, the bear was yanked out from under his palm; at the same time, a piercing scream filled the room, and the entire mattress moved.

Rock bolted upright, panic consuming him.

Lyla was next to him, sitting up, breathing heavily. For a moment, she stared at him, fear making her eyes wide.

He slowly reached out and cupped her cheek. "Nightmare?" He realized he must have been asleep a while because the sun was starting to come up.

She blew out a breath and nodded. "Sorry."

"It's okay, Baby girl." He tucked her hair behind her ear. "Understandable."

"That guy…" She shuddered.

"He's gone now. He can't hurt you."

"What if he comes back? What if he still thinks I have something of his?"

"He doesn't know where you are. I won't let him get near you, Little Lyla." He set his hand on her shoulder. "Lie down, Baby girl. Turn onto your other side." He guided her back to the mattress and rolled her away from him before wrapping his arms around her and spooning her.

"Deep breaths. I've got you." He stroked her hair, her arm, her hip.

She snuggled into him. "Rock…" She patted around on the mattress.

Confused, he gave her hand a squeeze. "I'm right here."

"No… The bears."

He chuckled. "Ah." He lifted onto his elbow and looked around until he found the two stuffies, reached out to snag them, and tucked them in her arms. "I think you'll need to name them something other than Rock. I'm going to get confused."

She gasped. "You can't give stuffies new names. Rock has been with me for years. That's madness."

He chuckled, loving the way it felt to laugh with her. "Good point. Maybe Rocky? Or Rock Two and Three?"

She giggled. "I don't think that will work, either."

Fuck, the sound of her laughter was musical. He pulled her closer, if that was even possible. If he had his way, he would never let her go. "How's your head, Little one?"

"Mmm. It's okay."

"And your arms?" He stroked gently over her bicep.

"Fine. Can I ask you something?"

"Lyla, you can ask me everything."

"Have you been in Shadowridge all these years?"

"Yes, Little one. Always. Except for the few months I was gone for my internship. I came home after that; took a job in town and a role in the MC. I've been here all my life."

She didn't respond.

He had a million questions for her. "Can I ask *you* something?"

"Mmm-hmm."

"Do you still sketch?"

"Yeah."

"Did you get your education degree?"

"Yes. I taught art in a high school for thirty years. I retired a few years ago."

"Retired, huh?" That was good news. Maybe she didn't have to be somewhere specific after she sold the house.

"Thirty years is long enough to deal with teenagers. Trust me."

He chuckled. "I can imagine. I was certainly glad when my kids exited that phase of life."

"I'm sorry about your wife," she whispered. "That must have been hard."

"It was, but I had the club for support and to help me out. My kids are good humans. I'm very lucky." He stroked her arm again, loving the goosebumps that rose. "I'm sorry things didn't work out with your husband."

She sighed. "Yeah. I don't think I was fully invested."

Because of me? That was crazy thinking. It was possible she hadn't thought of Rock a single time in those years, but he sort of liked to think no one had been able to measure up to him. Very caveman of him.

Rock buried his face in her hair and inhaled deeply. Her

scent hadn't changed. She used the same shampoo or something similar. He never wanted to take a break to exhale.

"Where do you live?"

"I moved to Florida to be near my parents after I retired. I have a condo a few miles from them. My mother is in poor health, but my father manages fine."

"And Jackson?"

"He lives in New York. He's divorced. Two adult children. Living life. I guess you didn't stay in contact with him?"

"No. I never saw him again after your parents moved away."

"It was hard in those days. No cell phones. No internet."

"Yes." He kept touching her, stroking her arm. It was soothing. He was afraid to ask the hard questions, so he didn't. Not yet. They would have to talk about the difficult things eventually, but not now.

She threaded her fingers with his—the arm he had stretched under her neck.

"Were those sketchpads I saw in your satchel?"

"Yeah." She twisted her neck to meet his gaze in the dim light. "Don't look at them," she demanded.

He furrowed his brow. "You still don't like anyone to see your work?" That was one of the first things she'd told him when they'd met.

"No. It's... My sketches are really just doodles. They're personal. I don't like to share."

"I bet you're an amazing artist. Too bad you keep it hidden."

"People *have* seen my art. After all, I taught it for thirty years. Just not my sketchpads."

"Ah. I'd like to see some of your work someday."

"Maybe. I don't sell it or anything, but I do have some of my own artwork on the walls of my condo."

"Oh, that's nice. Maybe you could paint something for my house."

"Mmm," she responded noncommittally.

"Does your head hurt? Do you want some more Tylenol?"

"I'm okay for now."

Talking to her was so easy. They'd rarely had the opportunity to just sit and chat back then. Occasionally, they'd have a few minutes together when her brother left the house to run out and pick up pizza, or when Rock came by early and her brother wasn't home. He'd made that happen as often as he could without it seeming weird to anyone, but not often enough.

After a bit of silence, Lyla spoke again. "I can't believe someone attacked me."

"I can't either. Crime is pretty low around here. I'm going to make some calls tomorrow and try to track that guy down. I don't like the idea of you having to look over your shoulder."

"Can you drop me off at the house in the morning? And maybe wait with me until Ink and Breaker get there?"

Rock scooted back a few inches and rolled Lyla onto her back so he could look into her eyes. "Baby girl, I'm not leaving you *anywhere*. If you want to go to the house, I'll take you to the house. If you want to go to the store, I'll take you to the store. If you want to get your nails done, I'll drive you and wait."

Her eyes went wide. "I can't ask you to do that."

"You didn't ask me. That's just how it is." He obviously hadn't made it clear that he had no intention of ever letting her out of his sight again. In truth, he realized he hadn't said that at all. He'd simply thought it. He might freak her the fuck out if he laid down the law like that.

"Surely you have stuff to do? A job? Club business? Family obligations?"

"Lyla, the moment I stepped into your house, you shot to number one on my priority list and knocked everything else down in importance. I don't have a traditional job. I worked for the city for many years, but I medically retired after my heart attack. I used to have a greater role in the club, but they no longer need me every hour of every day. My kids are grown adults. God bless Kade for chasing Remi around. She's a handful as a Little. And Atlas has his own handful, Carlee. Any stuff I had to do isn't important. I'll be stuck to you like glue."

She held his gaze and swallowed hard. "You can't mean that," she finally whispered.

"Every. Word."

She blinked. It was obvious she was stunned. Good. He didn't mind her being stunned. He wanted to be perfectly clear how he felt. In fact, fuck it, he would flat-out tell her.

He dropped a hand on the other side of her body, effectively pinning her on her back without touching her. "Lyla, I've wracked my brain a million times, trying to figure out what happened between us all those years ago. At the time, I spent months wondering and worrying. I couldn't understand why you disappeared and never came back. I beat myself up, trying to remember if I'd said something or done something to chase you away. I came up blank every time.

"I waited. I waited for over a year, pacing my apartment. When my lease was up, I renewed it for another year so you could easily find me. I checked in with the clubhouse every few days, asking if you'd called there, if you'd come by. Nothing. Always nothing. At the end of the following summer, a few of my associates dragged me to a bar, got me shitfaced, and told me it was time to move the fuck on. So, I did. It took a while, but I finally did. I had no way to find you. You were gone. You weren't coming back. I had to let you go and live my life. And I did.

"I lived. I stuffed the memory of you to the back of my brain and dated. I eventually met and married Kathy. We had a great life. And then she was gone. I'd lost two loves. I couldn't take something like that happening to me again, so I shut down and closed my heart off to other women.

"Now, my first love has suddenly shown up and flipped me on my ass. I know we have a million things to say to each other, but I'll be damned if I'll let you slip out of my hands again. I won't. Seeing you… It's like no time has passed at all. It's like the light has come back on in my world, and I don't want it to go out again.

"I don't care that you've been in my arms for less than twelve hours. I don't care what you have going for you in Florida. I'm not letting you go again. If you don't want to stay in Shadowridge, we'll go to Florida. Or Africa. Or fucking Thailand. I don't give a fuck where.

"So, no. I won't be dropping you off at your house and leaving you there with Ink or Breaker or any other of my brothers. I'd have heart palpitations if I left your side, worrying about you and freaking the fuck out. I don't know why you left without a word. I don't even care anymore. I only care that you're back, and I know you feel the same connection. I see it in your eyes. You sleep with the fucking stuffie I gave you when you were eighteen, for Christ's sake. You're mine, Lyla. For the rest of our lives, you're mine."

His heart was racing faster than ever, but nothing hurt. His ticker was fine. He hadn't felt this alive in years. The emotional exertion made him pant. He stared at her with the most serious, fierce expression he could paste on his face.

If she argued, he would counter everything she shot at him until he got her to see reason. She was his woman. His first love. His Little girl. His life partner. His last love.

After long seconds, she lifted her arms, snaked them around his neck, and pulled him toward her. Her gaze shifted to his lips. *Thank fuck.*

Rock cupped her head and brought his lips to hers, kissing her with all the passion he'd felt both then and now, kissing her like she was the last sip of water he would ever get, kissing her with his entire heart on his sleeve. Because his heart was hers.

The kiss lasted forever. When he finally pulled back, they were both breathing as though they'd run a marathon. He stared down into her eyes.

"Is it my turn to speak?" she asked, giving him a sweet smile.

"You can say anything to me," he promised.

She licked her lips. "I don't want to talk about why I didn't come back yet. I'm not ready. Let me process it for a while."

He nodded. He could live with that.

"But I believe you. I'm also willing to try this… Whatever this is. I wouldn't be able to turn you down if I wanted to. You had a magnetic pull on me from the moment you stepped into my basement when I was sixteen, and that pull did not lessen with time. I felt it the second I heard your voice last night. It's just as strong now as it was then. However, let's not get carried away. Let's feel each other out, get to know each other, and see if we have chemistry."

He smirked. "Baby girl, we have the most powerful chemistry on Earth." He cupped her face and kissed her again. Briefly, this time.

"Okay, maybe chemistry isn't the right word. Maybe our wants and desires don't align. Maybe our values aren't in sync. We don't know each other anymore. Let's take a step back and get to know each other."

He gave a sharp nod. "Little girl, I'll wait until the end of time for you to realize we're perfect together if that's what you need. As long as you agree to this exploration without leaving my side. That's my stipulation."

She held up a finger between them. "First things first. I'm not remotely sure I'm capable of being the Little girl you think I am. My only experience with any sort of Dom/sub relationship was the night we spent together. I've read a lot. I've researched it. But I have zero experience. I've never even been to a fetish club. So, be patient with me while I figure that out. I can tell dominance is in your blood, even without you pointing it out. I can also tell that you're a Daddy Dom. If I'm not feeling it, and I can't be the Little girl you crave, you have to be able to walk away."

He grabbed the finger she was shaking in front of him and brought it to his lips to kiss it. He had no concerns about her submission, but he would humor her and let her figure it out. "Agreed."

She lifted a brow. "Really? That was easy."

"That was me being cocky. There's a difference."

She giggled. Fuck, he loved that sound. He kissed her finger again. "I know you. I know the submissive in you needs nurturing. I'm not worried. What else do you want to throw at me? Bring it on. I can take it."

She drew in a breath. "I'll let you follow me around because I'm freaked out about what happened last night, but I need you not to rush me."

"I can agree to that, but you'll sleep in my bed either here or at the club from now on."

She nodded. "And I can agree to that as long as you don't pressure me to have sex."

"I won't pressure you."

She gave him a shove and slid out from under the covers.

He watched, wondering what was going on in her head as she stood next to the bed, wearing nothing but his T-shirt. She spun around, planted her hands on the mattress, and looked him in the eyes.

"You make my blood pump, Rock Monroe. You did then, and you still do now. I could pull this shirt off and let you ravage me—and I have no doubt you'll wear me down in less than a day—but you're a possessive Dominant, and I know you'll get even more bossy and controlling after I let you fuck me senseless. I remember what that feels like. I could feel your touch inside and outside my body for weeks. The memory of your hands and mouth on me distracted me for years. I woke up in a cold sweat many times, touching myself without even realizing what I was doing. I've masturbated to visions of you my entire life. Give me time to catch my breath and wrap my head around this before you take over my body."

He gave her a wicked grin, feeling pretty fucking good about himself. "As much time as you want, Baby girl."

She groaned. "You're not going to make it easy, are you?"

"Never."

She rolled those pretty eyes. "May I please take a shower, Master?"

He rose so fast that she jumped back. In seconds, he was on his feet, stalking her until she backed into the wall. He didn't touch her, but he once again pinned her anyway with a hand on either side of her head. He stared into her eyes. "You may take a shower. Don't forget to put your shampoo and girly shit in there before you start. I want you to smell like whatever floral flavor that shit is. Not my crap."

She nodded.

"And, Baby girl…"

"What?" Her voice wobbled. Good. He wanted her a little off-kilter. He liked it. "You won't call me Master. When you're ready, you will call me Daddy. There has never been anything sweeter in my life than the memory of you calling me Daddy. I can't wait to hear that word from your lips again. Until then, Sir or Rock will do. Understood?"

She swallowed, held his gaze, and firmly stated, "Yes, Sir," right before she ducked under his arm and slid from the room.

He didn't move for long seconds. His cock was harder than it had been in years. She'd just called him Sir, and she hadn't done so with a snarky voice.

She'd meant it.

When he finally shoved off the wall and stepped out of the room, rubbing his cock over the front of his shorts, he realized he had one more stipulation he wanted to make.

He stepped up to the bathroom door and knocked. "Lyla?"

"Yes?"

"I'm probably a far bossier Daddy Dom than you can even imagine. I will impose rules on you that will make your pussy so wet you won't be able to sit still. We'll get to those rules later, but I'm going to insist that you follow one of them starting right now."

"Rock…" she groaned.

"Little Lyla, I'm serious."

"Fine. What is this rule?"

"Do not touch that sweet pussy of yours any more than absolutely necessary. I don't know how often you masturbate or what you usually need to do to get off, but it stops now. Your orgasms are mine, starting this minute. Understood?" If she wanted to wait to have sex, he would give her as much time as she needed, but she sure as fuck wasn't going to lock herself in the bathroom, close her eyes, and picture him while she rubbed her pussy. Fuck, no.

Something clattered to the floor. It didn't sound like it broke. Maybe a brush or something.

"Lyla…"

"Yes, Sir," she responded.

"Good girl. Enjoy your shower. There's Tylenol in the medicine cabinet. Take some. I'll make breakfast."

His cock was too hard to walk straight as he stepped away, but he was feeling pretty good about himself, too. Smug.

Lyla was back.

Now, he just needed to help her see that she was his and he would never let her go again.

CHAPTER
TEN

Lyla trembled as she stared at her brush on the floor. She couldn't pick it up because she was gripping the edge of the vanity to keep from collapsing. Her head was spinning.

She was in Rock Monroe's home, in his bathroom, and he'd just ordered her not to masturbate. *Holy shit.*

Seconds ticked by while she waited to regain her composure. Her ears were ringing. Her hands were shaking. Her panties were soaked.

She finally pulled the T-shirt over her head and dropped it in the hamper. She put her panties in there, too. Why not? Might as well mix her clothes with his. She stared at her panties on top of his pile for a long time. It felt incredibly intimate.

Was she really going to do this? Stay with Rock, sleep in his bed, accept his protection…let him into her body?

That last part was inevitable. She hadn't been exaggerating when she pointed out it would probably take less than a day to spread her legs for him. He was potent. It didn't matter what was left unsaid between them. Nothing mattered except their undeniable chemistry.

She'd give anything to have him inside her. She'd lived off the memories for four decades. Maybe it hadn't been as good as she remembered, but it didn't matter because she could already tell it would be better now.

They'd barely been more than kids back then. She'd been a virgin. He'd been so gentle and caring with her. She doubted most women could speak so highly about their first time with a man. He'd made it magical and perfect.

But they were older now. They'd had sex with other people. Even if it had been a while, it was like riding a bike, wasn't it? Granted, she hadn't had any amazing experiences compared to the one night with him. She'd never called anyone Daddy. She'd never been with anyone who wasn't vanilla.

Hell, she could already sense that sex with Rock would flip her world over the same way it had the first time. Was it because they had some strange irrational chemistry, or was it just him? Rock. Was he always that good of a lover?

Lyla turned on the shower, waited for it to heat up, and stepped over the edge of the tub. It felt good to have warm water washing down her body. She winced several times as she washed her hair—every time she touched the back of her head—and her arms were sore. Lifting them was a chore, but every moment under the hot water felt amazing.

Next, Lyla reached for her razor. She decided to shave not just her legs but her pussy, too. She did so every few weeks, but considering the possibility that she might end up naked with Rock…

It wasn't until she was done with her shower and had combed out her hair that she realized she didn't have any clothes in the bathroom. She wrapped the towel around her and stepped into the living room.

Rock was at the stove, and he spun around to face her. His eyes went wide, and he stared for a few seconds before speaking. "I put your suitcase on the bed. It took every ounce of willpower I don't usually possess not to open it and put every-thing in drawers. Just so you know."

She chuckled. "So controlling."

"Yes. I cleared out one side of the dresser for you."

She inhaled deeply. "It smells so good in here."

"Please tell me you aren't vegan or something. You didn't mention it last night with the chicken soup."

"Nope. No special dietary requirements. I like most things. My stomach is growling now that I smell bacon."

"Breakfast is almost ready, Little Lyla. You're welcome to come to the table in that towel if you'd like." He grinned.

She rolled her eyes and headed into the bedroom, shutting the door behind her. She wasn't stupid. She knew he would see every inch of her soon, probably by tonight, considering how weak she felt about keeping her distance from him, but he didn't need to watch her get dressed this morning.

Putting on a bra proved to be a challenge. Her biceps were very sore. They were also turning purple in some places. She put a long-sleeved shirt on to cover them. She didn't need to watch Rock growl every time he saw the bruises, nor did she want to field questions from everyone she saw.

Fully dressed, including jeans and tennis shoes, she exited the bedroom. The table was covered with plates of food.

"How many people are you expecting for breakfast?" she asked as she joined him.

"I thought you might be hungry. Plus, I wasn't sure what your favorite breakfast foods were, so I went overboard."

"I am starving, and just so you know, I'm going to eat some of everything. Also, I'm impressed with your culinary skills."

He shrugged. "The kids were still young when Kathy died. I had to learn to be a Mom and a Dad really fast. I had to become domestic. They had to eat. I'm never going to win any cooking awards, but I'm pretty good with breakfast food."

She closed the distance and wrapped her arms around him.

"I'm really sorry about your wife." She'd said so already, but it couldn't hurt to tell him again. It must have been rough raising the kids on his own, even if he did have the help of the MC.

He hugged her back, burying his face in her hair and inhaling. She liked it when he did that. It made her feel special. "Thank you. Can I just say how glad I am that you're here?"

"I'm glad I'm here, too," she whispered, tipping her head back to look at him.

"We should eat before it gets cold. If I don't release you immediately, I'm going to end up pinning you to the wall and kissing you senseless again."

"You seem fond of kissing against the wall," she responded, clenching her legs together at the same time. It didn't take much for him to make her horny. Nearly everything he said was filled with sexual innuendo.

Rock released her and pulled out a chair. "Sit, Little Lyla."

She giggled. "I'm struggling to feel small."

"Not small, Little." He pushed her chair in.

"I know what you mean, but it's foreign to me."

He bent over and kissed the top of her head. "It won't be for long. When we go to the clubhouse, you'll be surrounded by Littles. They'll rub off on you and have you joining their antics in no time."

"Antics?"

He chuckled as he sat. "Little girls thrive on being naughty. You'll see."

"Mmm. Naughty, how?" She took a serving spoon from him and started filling her plate. But when she looked up at him and found his jaw tight, she handed the spoon back to him. "You want to do this, don't you?"

He smiled at her and took the spoon. "It's how I'm wired, Baby girl."

She waved toward the food. "Go ahead. I feel like a princess. If that's what it means to be Little, I won't argue."

"I want you to feel like a princess every day of your life, Lyla."

She noticed he'd already poured her a glass of juice. After picking it up, she took a long drink.

By the time she set the cup down, Rock had filled her plate and was sliding it in front of her. "Eat as much as you want."

She reached for her fork. "Can I feed myself?" she joked.

He leaned over and gripped her chin. "I'd love nothing more than to feed you myself, Baby girl. Don't tempt me. It was difficult for me to pull out an adult place setting. At the MC, most of the Little girls eat from plastic plates and use sippy cups."

She inhaled deeply. She had a lot to learn. "You don't mess around with age play, do you?"

"No."

"Rock..." She seriously worried she couldn't be what he needed. She was madly attracted to him, and she wanted him to strip her naked and make her see stars. But could she be Little? That was an uncertainty.

He set a hand over hers. "Don't worry about it right now. One hour at a time. We'll go to the clubhouse after you're done dealing with the house. You can meet my brothers and their Littles. If it's too overwhelming, we won't stay long."

She nodded. "Okay." She took a bite of hashbrowns and moaned as she chewed. When she glanced at Rock, she found him gripping his fork tightly, staring at her, his face stiff.

"If you're going to make noises like that while you eat, all bets are off. Fuck breakfast."

She swallowed and wiped her lips with her napkin. "Sorry. It's good. You sell yourself short. You're a great cook."

"You might recall I'm a great eater, too. That noise is going to have to be reserved for when my face is between your legs, Little Lyla."

Heat rushed up her body. Her cheeks were so hot she

thought they would catch fire. She'd give anything to be reminded about how it felt to have Rock's mouth on her pussy. She wanted that. She'd been reunited with him for about four waking hours. Mauling each other was a horrible idea. Wasn't it?

CHAPTER
ELEVEN

"Are you sure about this?" Lyla asked Rock two hours later as they stood in his driveway.

Rock wrapped an arm around her and pulled her into his side. He'd just handed the keys to her rental to Storm, the club VP. Another member, Blade, had dropped Storm off at Rock's house so he could return Lyla's car.

"You don't need a rental car, Baby girl," Rock stated. "I have both a car and a bike. I can only drive one at a time. Besides—" He pulled her closer and faced her, "—you're not going anywhere alone until that guy is caught. What would we do with three vehicles?"

She blew out a long breath and nodded.

He knew he was pushing her. He couldn't stop himself. Part of him was simply being practical, but another part was feeling more possessive and controlling than he'd ever felt before.

Storm pulled away with her rental, and Blade followed him.

Lyla slumped against Rock. "You're rushing me."

"Mmm." He cupped her face and kissed her. "Is my cock still in my pants?"

She rolled those pretty eyes.

"Now, we can take my car or my bike."

"Bike," she responded without hesitation.

"How many times have you been on a bike?"

"Twice."

His brows shot up. "Baby girl, you were on *my* bike twice."

"Yep."

He set his forehead against hers.

"And I loved it. It was exhilarating. I want to do it again."

"Are you sure you feel up to it? You'll have to hold on to me tight. Your arms are bruised."

"The bruises only hurt if you touch them. Don't grab my biceps, and we'll be fine."

It was a gorgeous day out. Chilly, but not too chilly to ride the bike. "All right, but you're wearing my cut. I don't want you to get cold."

"I can't take your jacket. I have my own. I'll go grab it."

He shook his head and led her back into the house. "Baby girl, I have more than one." He grabbed two off the hooks inside the kitchen and held one up to help her into it.

She tucked her nose under the front and inhaled deeply. "Smells like you."

Fuck, she was sexy. Everything she did was sexy. Every movement. But right now, she was damn gorgeous wearing his cut. She'd never done that before.

"Got everything you need, Little Lyla?"

She grabbed her satchel. "Yep. Phone, ID, credit cards, sketchpad. I'm good."

As badly as Rock wanted her behind him on his bike, he was certain his dick was going to be hard the entire time. His girl was going to flatten her chest to his back, wrap her arms around him, and hold on. There was no better feeling in the world.

Back outside, he grabbed a spare helmet from his saddlebag and secured it over her head, snapping it under her chin. "I'll mount first, then you grab onto me and swing your leg over behind me." He tucked her satchel in the saddlebag.

"Got it."

Seconds later, his Little girl was plastered to his back, her arms tight around his chest. He could get used to this. Hopefully she would enjoy riding with him and want to do so often.

Too bad her parents' house was only a few miles from his. He didn't get to spend nearly as much time riding with her as he would like, but she needed to meet Ink and Breaker at the house and let them in.

"Holy shit," Lyla muttered as he parked in her driveway and turned off the engine.

He twisted to look at her. "Language, Little girl."

Ignoring his reprimand, she looked around. "Why are so many members of the MC here, Rock?"

"Safety, Baby girl." He helped her dismount before doing the same.

"Don't you think this is a bit overboard?"

"Nope. I think my Little girl was attacked inside this house last night. I'm not taking any chances with her safety." He took her hand and led her to the front porch.

King stood by the door. He took Lyla's keys from Rock and turned to unlock it. "I'll check inside. Be right back." King disappeared.

Rock tucked Lyla into his side and hugged her close. "You okay, Little Lyla?" he murmured into her ear.

"I think so. Just overwhelmed. I don't know what I would do without your help today. There's no way I could have returned to the house and picked up where I left off."

"Well, you don't have to. I'm here."

King returned to the entrance. "It's all clear." He smiled and held out a hand to Lyla. "Nice to meet you. I'm King. You must be Lyla."

"Yes, Sir," she muttered. She lowered her gaze to the logo on his shirt. "Are you a firefighter?"

"Yep." He rubbed his eyes. "A very tired one."

Lyla's eyes widened. "Oh. I'm sorry. Did you just get off a rotation?" It was adorable that she was so concerned about others.

King chuckled. "No, but I met and claimed a certain Little girl named Ella recently, so I haven't been getting enough sleep between rotations." He winked at Lyla and lowered his voice. "Not that I'm complaining."

Rock took her hand and led her inside.

Lyla leaned close to him and whispered, "Does everyone know who I am?"

"Yeah. I didn't tell anyone except Atlas before I headed over here to see you last night, but I had to get the MC involved after your attack, Little one. None of them know our history yet. I'm sure they're curious, but they're too polite to the old guy to bombard me with questions."

"You're not old," she quipped. "If you are, then so am I, and I refuse to be old, so stop saying that."

He squeezed her hand and continued through to the kitchen, where he set her satchel on the counter. "I'll do my best, but I gotta warn you, the guys will call me old man anyway. I can't stop them."

Lyla glanced at the cooler and winced. "Shoot. I meant to go to the store this morning and get more supplies. Lunch and drinks."

Rock opened the fridge and laughed when Lyla gasped. "I sent a few guys to do that for you this morning."

"But I wanted to pay for it!" she exclaimed.

Rock chuckled. "Baby girl, that's not happening. It was kind of you to get Ink and Breaker lunch yesterday, but that was a one-time thing."

She put her hands on her hips. "You can't do that, Rock. I have to pay for the people working on my house."

He closed the distance and stalked her until she backed up against the wall. He loved the way her breath hitched as he closed in on her. "Baby girl, people have work done on their house every day. They don't buy the workers' lunch."

She pouted. "Well, they should. It's kind."

He cupped her face. "I love that you're kind. Most people aren't. I've got lunch, Little Lyla. You can pay for the home improvements. A bunch of the guys are going to pitch in and get the job done. I don't like you hanging around this house any longer than necessary."

"Okay," she murmured as her hands came to his front and slid under his cut to press against his chest.

He tipped her head back farther and narrowed his gaze at her. "If you were planning to leave town the moment they were done, I'll send them all away now and slow the process to a crawl."

She grinned. "That *had* been my plan. I figured it would take a few weeks; then I could put the house on the market and leave. I don't need to be here while it's up for sale."

He growled. "Lyla…"

She giggled. "I promise I won't bolt immediately just because the job is done." She slid her hands higher, wrapping her fingers around his shoulders. "I met this guy…"

He smirked. "I'll cuff you to the bed at night and not let you leave my sight during the day if you're planning on bolting, Little girl." He knew this was mostly banter. She was teasing him. But he realized it was true that she had planned to leave. She hadn't known he would even be in town or available when she arrived. Staying in Shadowridge hadn't been on her bingo card.

He fully intended to change her mind.

"Mmm. I might like the idea of being cuffed to the bed, but you don't have to do it all night. I'm not going to run."

Rock sobered completely and pressed his body against hers. "You ran once. Took me nearly four decades to get you back. It will kill me if you do it again."

She licked her lips. "Neither of us can be certain things will work out between us. It hasn't been a full day. We might have conflicting views on something that would be a deal breaker."

He shook his head. "We won't."

She rolled her eyes.

Rock slid his hands down to squeeze her bottom. "If I spanked you every time you rolled your eyes at me, you wouldn't be able to sit for a week."

She shivered delightfully.

He groaned. "My girl likes the idea of being spanked."

"Maybe."

"Seems like you've been living a very vanilla lifestyle. Has anyone spanked you, Little Lyla?"

"Yes. You did. I remember it well."

His chest tightened. *Fuck me.* Part of him felt sad that she'd spent all these years ignoring her Little. Most of him was fist-pumping from the realization that all of her kinky experiences would be his. He would be the one to reintroduce her to a life she'd turned her back on. He was so anxious to do so that he wanted to drag her into one of the bedrooms, lock the door, take her over his knees, and spank her bottom until she writhed. He wanted to follow that up by finger-fucking her sweet pussy until she screamed.

Not here. Not now.

Lyla clenched her butt cheeks in his palms. "I should go talk to Ink and Breaker. See if they need anything."

Rock gently kissed her lips because he couldn't resist. "Okay, but this conversation isn't over."

She kissed him back. "None of our conversations are over, Rock."

Damn straight.

"I need to talk to some of my brothers. You deal with the renovations."

"Okay."

When he eased back, she grabbed his hips and moved with him. "For the record, I'd rather be alone with you right now, and I suddenly feel like a teenager again."

He cupped her bottom again. "Me, too, Little Lyla. Me, too."

CHAPTER
TWELVE

"You got it. No problem. We'll comb the entire place."
Lyla stepped into the kitchen from the basement to find Rock and three other members of the Guardians seemingly in a meeting. She only caught those last three sentences. "What's going on?" She looked around at each of them, noting the furrowed brows and serious expressions.

Dipping into her brain, she tried to remember who each of them were. She'd met so many people this morning that it was hard to keep track. It seemed like half the MC had come by or was working on her house.

Lyla was pretty sure the men in the huddle were Steele, the club president; Kade, the enforcer; and Atlas, the treasurer and Rock's son. She knew him for certain. It was still eerie looking at him. He was like a young Rock.

Rock reached out a hand toward her. "Come, Little one."

She went to him, feeling out of sorts. It was one thing for him to Daddy her in private, but it felt strange in front of all these men, including his son. Even though she knew all of them were Daddies and had wives and girlfriends of their own, it wasn't a lifestyle she was accustomed to.

Rock pulled her in front of him and wrapped his arms

around her from behind, claiming her hard. "Do you mind if the club knows how we know each other?"

She shook her head. It would probably be easier if they knew the truth than assuming she was some hussy he'd met last night.

He faced Steel and Kade. "My senior year of high school, I became good friends with a guy named Jackson. The first time I went to his house, I met this amazing girl who took my breath away."

Lyla giggled when Rock bent his head to kiss her neck. It was like he was telling them some sort of tragic love story. He kind of was. She looked at the men and rolled her eyes, hoping he didn't notice. Or maybe she didn't care if he noticed. She was kind of looking forward to the promised spanking. "He exaggerates. I have no idea what he saw in me. I was gangly with glasses and braces. My hair was stringy. My body was…immature."

The men chuckled.

"I'm sure Rock's version is different," Steele said.

Rock cleared his throat. "Don't think I didn't notice the eye roll, Little girl," he said sternly.

Lyla shivered in his arms. She wasn't used to PDA. He was wrapped around her in front of the most important people in his life. And she kind of liked it. Her husband had rarely touched her in front of other people. She hadn't even realized it kind of hurt her feelings until this moment.

It felt nice to be claimed.

Rock continued, "Anyway, Lyla was only sixteen at the time, so I kept my hands and thoughts to myself for two years. It wasn't until after she turned eighteen, right before her graduation, that we, uh…" He waved a hand through the air as he skipped the details.

She was glad. Her face was hot, and she was slightly worried about how his son was taking this information.

Atlas didn't look upset. He was smiling.

"Life was complicated, though. I had a summer internship in another town, and Lyla went away to college. We lost touch."

"Wait…" Atlas said, "You mean you never saw each other again?"

Lyla swallowed, tears welling up in her eyes. It sounded so tragic. Maybe it was.

Rock kissed her neck again. "Not until last night."

"Holy fuck, Dad." Atlas glanced back and forth between them. "You two look like you haven't even missed a beat."

"I feel kind of sad," Kade muttered.

Lyla took a deep breath and wiped her eyes, sucking back the tears. "I'm here now."

"Are you staying?" Steele asked.

Rock answered, "It hasn't even been a day. We have a lot of catching up to do."

Lyla was grateful for his response. The deflection. After a long silence, she repeated her initial question, "What were you all saying about combing the place?"

Rock turned her so she was against his side and looked down at her. "This house. We bumped heads about your attacker. He said, 'where is it?' That makes us think he hid something here in the house. Apparently, when he came back for it, it was gone, and he thinks you found it."

Steele nodded. "We've spoken to Ink and Breaker. They haven't seen anything out of the ordinary, and they haven't taken anything from the property."

She glanced at Rock. How could they be sure?

He must have read her expression. "They've been prospects with the Shadowridge Guardians for a while, Little one. They're good guys. We've never had a single issue with them. There's no way they would ruin their chances with the MC by stealing something from my woman's house and lying about it."

She nodded.

"Besides," Kade added, "if they had found something, and it was valuable, they would have left town, not shown up again today to keep working."

Kade had a point. "Right. Okay. So why bother combing the place? We already know it's not here, whatever *it* is."

Steele rubbed his beard. "We're looking for a hiding place, maybe a false wall behind a cabinet or space under a floorboard, something that could have been a hiding place. It isn't likely to be in plain sight."

Rock nodded. "Gabriel and Talon are talking to the neighbors to see if anyone has seen any suspicious activity since the last renters moved out. Maybe someone saw your attacker coming and going. If he's only been here in the middle of the night, though, it's likely no one would have seen him."

That was a good idea. Honestly, Lyla had been so consumed with Rock's appearance and her deep feelings for him that she hadn't stopped to consider the possibilities regarding her attacker. It was easier to put it out of her mind.

Kade shoved away from the counter he'd been leaning against. "Trust me. If there's anything remotely suspicious on this property, one of us will find it."

Rock tipped her chin back. "Do you remember any secret hidey-holes from your childhood?"

"No. I suppose we could ask Jackson, but he never told me about any secret compartments."

Rock held her gaze. "I think we should call Jackson anyway."

"Call Jackson about what? What's going on here?"

At the sound of her brother's voice, Lyla spun around so fast she nearly fell on her ass.

Jackson was entering the kitchen, flanked by two of the Guardians.

"Sorry, Pres," the one who'd introduced himself as Bear said, looking at Steele. "Didn't mean to interrupt. This guy says he's Lyla's brother."

When she locked eyes with her brother, Lyla ran across the room and threw her arms around Jackson. She hadn't seen him in almost a year. They didn't get together these days as often as they used to. "What are you doing here?" she asked as she leaned back, still holding his arms.

He smirked. "Mom and Dad guilted me into coming. They said it wasn't fair for me to leave you to take care of the house alone. I took a few days off work. I can't stay long, but I'm here." He looked around. "Why exactly is the entire Shadowridge Guardians MC here?"

Lyla stepped to the side. She was about to make some introductions when Jackson suddenly gasped.

"Rock? Holy shit. It's you." Jackson stepped toward his old friend and gave him a solid man hug.

"In the flesh," Rock stated as they parted. He took over the introductions, pointing around the room. "This is Steele, the club president. Kade, the enforcer. Atlas, the treasurer. He's also my son."

Jackson chuckled. "Shit, yes. I see the resemblance."

Rock turned toward the two guys who'd walked in with Jackson. "Bear, the club secretary. Storm, the VP."

Jackson shook everyone's hand. "And you're all here because…?"

Lyla explained, "The realtor recommended two guys, who happen to be prospects with the MC, to do some of the renovations around the house. I hired them. They spent yesterday tackling the blue carpet you put on the wall downstairs." She lifted her brows. "Did you seriously need to both staple and glue it? They had to remove the drywall to get it off."

Jackson cringed. "You removed my blue carpet?" he teased. "That was so innovative. I was so proud of myself for coming up with that. Early eighties acoustic magic. I can't believe it was still there."

Rock chuckled. "It was an eyesore in the eighties, and it

still was yesterday. I didn't have the heart to tell you back then."

Jackson set a hand over his heart as though he were offended. He turned back to Lyla. "And now the entire MC is here?"

"Not quite all of us," Rock continued. "Some shit went down."

Lyla was grateful he was taking over.

"What kind of shit?" Jackson glanced around.

Lyla touched his arm.

Rock cleared his throat. "A guy came in last night after Ink and Breaker left and attacked Lyla."

Jackson gasped and jerked his attention toward his sister. "What the fuck?"

Rock nodded. "Yeah, that's basically how we're all feeling. I'd found out Lyla was here, and it was a blessed coincidence that I stopped by within a minute of the attacker. I scared him off, but then I attended to Lyla instead of chasing him. He's still on the run."

"Did you call the police?" Jackson asked, his narrowed gaze on Lyla. "Are you okay?"

"I'm okay," she assured him. "Bumps and bruises. I'll be fine. Yes, we called the police."

Steele growled. "But our MC isn't too keen on waiting for the bureaucracy of the police department. Don't get me wrong, we have a symbiotic relationship. We help each other out from time to time, but the Guardians are usually faster to solve a crime. We don't…fill out paperwork, so to speak."

Lyla drew in a deep breath. She wasn't even going to ask what he meant by that. It was pretty evident. In fact, she took a step back and simply listened while Steele brought Jackson up to speed.

Jackson listened closely with a furrowed brow. "So, we're looking for a secret hiding place?"

"Yes," Kade confirmed. "Not sure it will be helpful since

whatever this guy might have stashed here obviously isn't there anymore, but perhaps we'll find a clue."

Jackson ran a hand through his hair and turned around in a slow circle before returning to face everyone. "I know where it is."

Lyla gasped. She hadn't expected that answer.

"You had a secret hiding place in your house?" Rock asked.

Jackson winced. "Yeah."

"How the hell did I not know about it?" Rock's voice wasn't angry. It was curious.

Jackson chuckled. "Oh, the irony."

Lyla looked back and forth between them. "Someone want to fill me in?"

Jackson started laughing. Within seconds, he bent at the waist and set his palms on his knees while he laughed even harder.

Lyla stared at both of them with raised brows. The rest of the guys simply waited with equally curious expressions.

Jackson smirked as he turned his attention back to Lyla. "Mom and Dad thought Rock was a bad influence on me."

"Yeah, so?" She'd known that. Her parents had tolerated Rock. They weren't mean people, but they struggled to look past the tattoos and the motorcycle and the leather. They never said a word, but they often pursed their lips. It was obvious they were leery.

Jackson shrugged. "So, I had weed. I smoked pot from time to time. I hid it from Mom and Dad." He nodded toward Rock. "This dude was too straight-laced for weed. He didn't approve, so I didn't mix my smoking habit with Rock."

Rock shook his head slowly.

Lyla started giggling. "That's hilarious."

"Did you ever finally smoke a doobie, man?" Jackson asked.

Rock rolled his eyes. "Yes. How about we get back to the subject at hand? Where's the hiding place?"

"And who else knew about it?" Steele asked.

Jackson froze, his face sobering. Finally, he slapped his forehead. "I know who attacked you."

Lyla's mouth dropped open. How the hell was that possible?

"Carl Houseman."

Lyla frowned. She recognized the name, but it took her a few seconds to remember who it was. "Carl? That sleazy guy with the stringy blond hair who sometimes came over?" She stopped talking abruptly when she suddenly put several pieces of the puzzle together. "His parents were the last people renting this house."

Jackson nodded. "Yep. They were good people. They didn't have a great relationship with Carl. I bet he was using the house to stash his shit, and then they inconveniently ended their lease and moved out."

"I vaguely remember Carl," Rock said. "I'll call the police and let them know our suspicions."

"So…" Kade added, "If he was keeping something in this house, where is it now?"

They all looked at each other. That was the million-dollar question.

One thing was for sure: Lyla was not going to hide her relationship with Rock from her brother. She'd been standing apart from Rock for several minutes now, and she didn't like it.

She moved into Rock's side, wrapped her arms around his middle, and kissed him on the lips before turning to face Jackson. "There's one more thing you need to know."

CHAPTER
THIRTEEN

Rock glanced over at his Little girl every few seconds as he drove toward the clubhouse. It had been a long day, and it was still light out. They'd gone home for a bit to trade the bike for the car. Rock was afraid it would be too chilly later tonight to bring his Little girl home on the bike. "You okay, Little one?"

She was chewing on her bottom lip, but she released it and sighed. "Yeah. I think so. Still trying to wrap my head around everything. I can't believe my brother had a secret hiding place for marijuana behind the vent in his bedroom."

Rock reached over and clasped her hand.

She jerked her gaze toward him. "I also can't believe you didn't smoke pot back then."

He chuckled. "I wasn't much of a rule breaker. No one believed that about me. It's hard for people to look past the tattoos and leather."

"Including my parents."

He shrugged. "I couldn't blame them. All I could do was always be polite and courteous around them. I didn't want to do anything to get out of their good graces." He squeezed her hand.

"Because of me."

"Yes." It was always because of Lyla. Everything he did in those days was because of Lyla.

She leaned her head back against the seat. "Did you see the look on my brother's face when I kissed you?"

Rock's entire body shook from laughter. Thank goodness he was at a traffic light. "I thought we were going to have to put his eyeballs back into the sockets."

"It took him damn near half an hour to wrap his head around the fact that we'd had a thing for each other back then. I wasn't sure we'd hidden it that well. I wasn't sure *I'd* hidden it that well."

Rock lifted her hand to his lips and kissed her knuckles. "Apparently, we did. I bet he picked up a pizza, checked into the motel, and he's now staring at the wall, trying to think about the signs he missed."

"I kinda feel bad about leaving him to his own devices tonight."

"I know. But we offered."

"It's better this way. I don't think I can juggle adding my brother to our evening. I'm freaking out enough about meeting your daughter and all the other members of your club."

"You've met damn near all of them, Little Lyla. It's the girls you haven't met yet. And they will welcome you with open arms. They're the nicest women you'll ever meet."

She sighed heavily. He knew she was nervous. He couldn't blame her, but they had to rip this bandage off. He was confident she had a strong Little side and always had. She just hadn't had the opportunity to let it out and explore.

He pulled into the compound, parked, and shut off the engine before turning to face her. "If you get overwhelmed, we'll leave."

"I'll be fine."

He kissed her fingers one more time before sliding out of the car and rounding to her side to let her out. Threading their fingers together, he led her toward the side entrance, so they entered into the main living space, the common area.

It was filled with people, and the noise level was high, but as soon as someone spotted them entering and grabbed the next person's arm and so on, a hush fell over the group.

Remi was the first to step between everyone and make her way toward Rock and Lyla, smiling warmly as she approached.

Lyla stiffened by his side, but Remi didn't say a word. Instead, she took Lyla in her arms and hugged her tightly. "Welcome," she said just loud enough for Rock to hear. Bless his sweet daughter.

Remi was wearing all black, including her combat boots. She had high pigtails with black ribbons, black eyeliner, and black lipstick.

Rock pulled Lyla back to his side. "Remi, this is Lyla. Lyla, this is my daughter, Remi. I forgot to mention she's in a goth phase," he teased.

Remi rolled her eyes. "Dad, it's not a phase. And besides, Kade doesn't mind. He likes it." She stuck her tongue out.

Kade joined them and tipped Remi's head back. "Did you just stick your tongue out *and* roll your eyes at your father?"

Remi shrugged. "Maybe."

"Lyla has been here two seconds. Did you want her to watch you get your bottom spanked before she's all the way through the door?"

Remi cocked her head to the side, giving Kade sass. "You wouldn't."

Kade set a hand on the back of her neck and turned her away. "We'll be back."

"Daddy!" Remi shouted.

Rock wasn't overly surprised by his daughter's behavior, but he was kind of shocked she pulled out all the stops so quickly.

What did surprise Rock was the fact that Lyla was covering her mouth and fighting a giggle.

He bent over to whisper in her ear. "Sorry about that. Welcome to the Shadowridge Guardians MC. The age play here is strong and abundant, especially now that so many Littles have joined us."

"I think I get it," she responded softly.

The other women started filing forward.

"So glad you're here. I'm Ivy, Steele's Little girl." She gave Lyla a hug. These girls were friendly with each other. They wouldn't give a formal handshake.

"I'm Carlee. You met my Daddy, Atlas, at the grocery store."

"My name is Harper. My Daddy is Doc."

This went on until all eleven of the women had introduced themselves. Rock was pretty sure there was no way Lyla would remember all their names, but she looked like she was trying to memorize them. He was so grateful for everyone and that they'd all rearranged whatever they'd had planned for tonight so they could be here to meet Lyla. It meant a lot to him.

He was one of the older members of the club, and he didn't have a specific role among the voting members any longer. Years ago, he'd been the secretary, but now he was simply respected for his age and the length of time he'd been a member.

The Littles were all dressed up, too. They had on pretty dresses, hair ribbons, and frilly socks. None of them were hiding who they were.

"Bear made mac and cheese," Ella told Lyla. "He's the best cook." She moaned as if she were currently eating his food.

"You're King's Little girl, right?" Lyla asked.

"Yep." Ella beamed. "Come on." She held out a hand. "I'll show you around the clubhouse."

King came up behind her and set his hands on her shoulders. "Do you think you should maybe ask Rock for permission before you drag Lyla away? Maybe he'd like to show Lyla around himself."

Ella lifted her gaze to Rock's. "Sorry, Rock. May I show Lyla around?"

Rock shifted his attention to Lyla, trying to gauge her reaction.

She smiled at him and reached up to kiss his cheek. "I'm okay. You don't have to hover. I'll be fine."

He set his palm on the back of her neck and kissed her hard on the lips. "Baby girl, I will hover for the rest of your life. Get used to it. But I'll let the Little girls show you around if you're okay with it. I'll be in the kitchen if you need to find me." He pointed across the room toward a door.

Lyla nodded. "Got it."

Ella took one of her hands. Sapphire, Blade's Little girl, took the other, and they were off.

Rock watched as they disappeared, praying he was doing the right thing. It wasn't as though Lyla was twenty and didn't know her mind. She was fifty-six. If she got uncomfortable, she would surely extricate herself from any situation.

"You dog," Storm said, slapping a hand on Rock's shoulder. "All these years…"

Apparently, word had gotten around. Rock didn't mind. It was actually easier for the rumor mill to have spread the details of his relationship with Lyla.

Faust joined them. "Has it really been forty years since you last saw her? Molly didn't believe that part."

Rock nodded. "It has. Well, thirty-eight. We lost touch." He didn't want to expound on that. He didn't have all the answers himself yet. There were things Lyla hadn't told him.

Talon stepped closer, holding a beer. "What matters is that she's here now."

Gabriel was next to join. "Is she planning to stay?"

Rock rubbed his beard. "We only reconnected last night. I don't know every eventuality yet."

"But you hope so," Atlas said.

"I do."

"Love matters more than location," Atlas added, lifting a brow. "I know that better than anyone. If she's your woman, you'll go to another planet with her to please her."

Atlas had come to town intending to help the club out with their finances and then returning to the big city where he was an accountant. Reuniting with Carlee had changed his plans, but Rock knew he would have done whatever was best for Carlee. At one point, it had looked like taking Carlee away from Shadowridge might have been the best option.

Rock was fucking glad Atlas had stayed and made a home here. They'd spent too many years apart.

But Atlas was also right. Love trumped everything. Even though it hadn't been a full twenty-four hours since he'd been reunited with Lyla, he knew in his heart he would never let her go again. He didn't even like that she'd left the room with the Littles.

His chest was tight, and he almost reached up to rub it but stopped himself. There was nothing wrong with his ticker. His heart, yes, but not its functioning. He didn't need half the MC harping on him about his health.

Elizabeth squeezed in between her Daddy, Talon, and Faust. She looked toward Rock, biting her lip.

"Is everything okay?" Rock panicked a bit.

"Yes. We were wondering if you would mind if we offered to lend Lyla some clothes. I mean, some Little clothes."

Rock smiled. "That's fine, but don't pressure her. She might not be ready for that." She might not ever be ready for that. It was a reality he was going to have to face. He truly believed she had a Little inside her, a side she'd buried for all these years, but it was also possible it was all wishful thinking on his part.

"We won't. Thanks, Rock." Elizabeth skipped away.

Talon groaned. "The skipping is a conspiracy between the Littles to get away with running in the house."

Doc chuckled. "I'm good with mandating they can't *skip* in the compound either if we all agree."

Faust shook his head. "The skipping is cute, plus it's hard for Molly to keep from running when she starts skipping, which gives me an excuse to spank her bottom."

Rock chuckled. Faust had a point.

Atlas slapped him on the back. "Let's see if Bear needs help in the kitchen. It will take your mind off things while we give the girls a chance to connect."

CHAPTER
FOURTEEN

Lyla felt like she'd fallen into a parallel dimension. Eleven women hovered around her, all dressed as though it were Halloween and they'd agreed to go as children.

Lyla had to remind herself over and over this was their way of life, not a costume party. She kept asking them to repeat their names so she could remember who they were and who their significant others were—their Daddies.

They showed her around the compound, including their various apartments. Apparently, many of the club members had rooms in the clubhouse. Some of them lived here full-time, and some lived in homes in the community—like Rock.

Remi came out of one of the apartments after a bit. She didn't look any different, but she did wince occasionally.

Elizabeth had left them, and she suddenly returned, skipping down the hall. "Rock said *yes*!" she exclaimed.

"Rock said *yes* to what?" Remi asked.

Lyla was wondering the same thing.

A woman named Eden—Lyla thought her Daddy was Gabriel—responded, looking at Lyla, "We thought you might like to borrow some clothes. You don't have to, of course. But if you wanted, we could lend you something."

Lyla swallowed, wondering what she meant. She hesitated a moment before it dawned on her. *Little* clothes. Dresses like they were wearing.

Remi reached out and touched her arm. "You don't have to," she repeated. "It's just… Whatever makes you feel more comfortable. We want you to feel welcome."

Lyla turned toward Remi. This was Rock's daughter. Rock had a daughter. And a son. It was suddenly all kind of overwhelming. Because Lyla had fled town and never come back, Rock had married another woman and had two kids.

Remi moved in front of Lyla, blocking her from everyone else. "Hey," she whispered.

A hushed murmur spread behind Remi.

Remi turned toward the others and said, "Give us a minute, yeah?"

"Of course," several of them responded at the same time.

Remi opened the door she'd come out of, took Lyla's hand, and gently pulled her inside. She shut the door behind them and led Lyla to a sofa. "I'm sorry," she said as they sat.

Lyla wiped her eyes. She hadn't realized tears had formed. "No. Don't be. It's not you. Shoot." She wiped them again. Damn tears. "I'm sorry. I don't know why I'm crying."

Remi rubbed her arm. "It's okay. We can be a bit much at times. We didn't mean to make you feel overwhelmed. It's just that…"

Lyla swallowed and looked at Remi. If Lyla had had a child, she would be Remi's age. But she hadn't.

Remi grabbed her hand. "Do you want me to get my dad?"

"No." Lyla swallowed back her emotions and shook her head. "No, please. I'm okay. Go on, what were you going to say? It's just that, what?"

Remi licked her lips. "Well, my Dad's been alone a long time. When we heard he'd met you… Well, we didn't know he'd already known you in the past. That didn't really matter. We were just… I mean, I… I was hoping he'd found someone. We all worry about him. Me. I worry about him the most. He's alone. And…" Remi's bottom lip quivered.

Lyla's tears fell again. She couldn't stop them. She pulled Remi into her arms and hugged the woman tightly. "I was worried you wouldn't want your dad to be with another woman."

Remi leaned back. "God, no. I've prayed he would meet someone for years. It's hard for him. He doesn't exactly subscribe to dating apps." She chuckled and swiped at tears again. "Where is a middle-aged widower supposed to find a Little?"

Lyla sniffled, smiling through the tears. "I'm not quite sure I'm Little. I haven't even thought about it since the last time I saw your dad."

Remi smiled. "When did you last see him? He didn't tell us all the details."

"The night of my prom. He…" Lyla took a deep breath. "I was so young." Lyla held up a finger. "Eighteen, though."

Remi giggled and rolled her eyes. "I was a teenager once. I'm not naïve."

Lyla drew in a deep breath. "Anyway, you don't want the gritty details about your dad, but the important thing is that my prom date turned out to be a douchebag. I was upset when I got home. Your dad was there, waiting for me. He comforted me."

Remi waved a hand between them. "Among other things. I get it. Skip that part."

Lyla chuckled. "It was the first and only time I acknowledged my Little side. Your dad left town for an internship a few days later, and then I went away to college. We never saw each other again."

"Why?"

Lyla sighed. "That's another story. Rock and I haven't discussed it yet."

"Okay. I understand. So, you're here. And you still like my dad."

Lyla smiled. More tears fell for whatever reason. She nodded. "I do. I *really* like your dad. It's like no time passed at all. It feels like I've been here weeks instead of one day."

Remi squeezed her hand. "Do you think you have a Little side?"

"I don't know. It's foreign to me right now. Rock thinks I do." Lyla reached up and thumbed a lock of Remi's hair. "You're so pretty. I'm so glad he got married and had you and Atlas."

"Do you have kids?"

"No. I couldn't have any. And I'm not sure I was cut out for motherhood anyway. I keep thinking if I hadn't left... If I had stayed with Rock..." She swallowed hard. "He wouldn't have you and Atlas."

Remi reached up and hugged her again. "You're here now. I know you're important to my dad. I want you to feel welcome here. Everyone wants you to feel welcome."

Lyla nodded. "I do. Thank you."

"If you want to borrow some clothes, I have some things that aren't black." Remi giggled. "But maybe it would be better if you stayed in your regular clothes tonight. Observe. Figure out what your style is."

"Well, I don't think it's going to be goth," Lyla teased.

They both laughed.

Remi winced when she leaned back.

Lyla cringed. "Do you like getting spanked?"

Remi grinned huge. "Love it. I'm sorry I misbehaved in front of you the moment you arrived. I couldn't resist. I knew Kade would spank me, and I was stressed. I really needed the outlet."

"Stressed about meeting me?"

Remi shrugged. "Partly."

Lyla was curious about spankings. "And you feel better after Kade spanks you?"

"Yes. Always. It's common in age play. Us Littles frequently get up to no good in order to get spanked. It's like a challenge. We've pulled some crazy stunts around here."

"I bet you have."

"Have you ever tried it? Spanking, I mean."

Lyla slowly nodded. "Once."

Remi giggled and covered her ears. "La la la. I can tell it was that night. Do *not* tell me about it."

They both fell into a fit of giggles again.

A knock sounded at the door.

Remi stood and went to open it.

It was Rock. Not surprising. He looked past his daughter. "Are you okay?"

Lyla nodded. "I'm good. Sorry. I just needed a minute."

Remi grabbed her dad's arm and rose up to kiss his cheek. "I love her, Dad." She slipped from the room and shut the door.

Rock leaned against the door. His brow was furrowed with concern. "I was panicking."

Lyla stood. "No need. I'm good. I promise."

"Did they scare you off?"

She came to him and set her hands on his shoulders. "No, Daddy," she said sarcastically. "They didn't. I'm still here."

He narrowed his gaze. "As nice as that sounds, don't say it until you mean it."

She set her forehead against his. "Okay," she whispered.

"The girls didn't talk you into getting changed," he pointed out.

"No." She slid her hands up his chest. "I don't think I'm ready for that, but I'm good. Don't worry."

"Do you want to stay for dinner or make a run for it? I won't be disappointed either way."

"Let's stay. I enjoy seeing the dynamic. I'm learning from them."

"Okay." He eased his hands up her back. "I didn't like you being out of my sight." He kissed her.

"I was always close," she murmured. "Is one of these apartments yours?"

"Yes. Wanna see it?" he teased.

"Will it cause us to miss dinner?"

"Yes." He didn't hesitate.

She giggled. "Maybe we should save that for another day."

"Bear went all out to impress you with dinner."

"Then we shouldn't disappoint him."

CHAPTER
FIFTEEN

ock frowned when Lyla rubbed her temples as he pulled into his driveway later that night. "Your head hurting?"

"Not really. It was just a long day."

"I think you need a bath, some snuggling, and some sleep."

He loved the way she groaned at the suggestion. "That sounds amazing."

Rock rounded the car, opened the door for her, and helped her out. Without a word, he guided her into the house and took her jacket. He cupped her face and took a chance. "Let me bathe you."

She swallowed and then nodded. "I'd like that."

Rock took her hand and walked toward the bathroom. It wasn't a huge bathroom. He'd never even thought about it. He'd lived here alone for a long time. He certainly didn't need a big bathroom. But maybe this house wasn't big enough for the two of them.

Please, God. Make this work. Let me spend the rest of my days with this woman.

Rock leaned over and turned on the water. He adjusted the temperature before putting the stopper in. When he turned back to look at Lyla, she was setting her jewelry on the vanity. She'd kicked off her shoes and placed them outside the bathroom, too.

When she reached for the hem of her shirt, he stopped her. "Let me, Baby girl," he murmured.

"Okay." She lifted her arms and allowed him to pull her shirt over her head.

As he dropped it in the hamper, he noticed her wincing slightly. He cringed, too, when he saw the bruises on her arms. He gently held her elbow and bent to kiss one bicep and then the other. "We'll catch him, Little Lyla. I promise."

He held her gaze while he unbuttoned her jeans. "You sure you're okay with this?"

She nodded and stepped closer. "I want your hands on me. I want to remember. I want to go back in time and redo it." Her voice wobbled.

He grabbed her belt loops and hauled her closer, kissing all over her cheeks. "Will you tell me why you left, Little one?" he whispered.

"Yes. Eventually."

"Okay. I'll respect that. We can't go back in time, but we have forever in front of us. It started last night. You're mine, Lyla." He didn't mean to growl, but it came out that way.

She nodded, though. "I'm yours. I was always yours."

He unzipped her jeans and pulled them down her legs, squatting to tug them off her feet one at a time while she held his shoulders. While he was still face-level with her pussy, he tucked his fingers in her panties and eased them over her hips.

She'd shaved. Everything. So fucking sexy.

He leaned forward and kissed her pussy, loving the way she moaned.

As he rose, he eased his hands slowly up her body and slid them around to unfasten her bra. Fuck, she was gorgeous. She was prettier than his memory had conjured. Sexier than she'd been when she'd been eighteen.

"Jesus..." he whispered. "I'm so fucking lucky."

She shivered. Her nipples stiffened. Hard rose-colored tips reached for him, fuller than they'd been all those years ago. She weighed a few more pounds than she had then, but her breasts were fantastic, still high and firm.

"You're staring," she murmured.

"I'm going to come in my jeans."

She giggled. "Take them off?"

He shook his head. "Not now. Let me wash you first." He took her hand and helped her into the tub.

His cock pressed hard against his fly, but he ignored it. He set a folded towel on the tile and dropped to his knees to wash his Little girl.

Lyla sighed contentedly and let him take care of her. She closed her eyes as he poured water over her head. It had been so long since he'd washed someone, but it felt like home. Like he'd been waiting for her, and now she was here.

He took his time, letting his hands gently scrub her scalp, paying close attention to not put too much pressure on the back of her head. He moved to her arms and legs and, finally, her torso and pussy.

They didn't speak while he washed her. It was a reverent experience. She parted her thighs for him and moaned softly when he touched her pussy with the washcloth.

When he was done, he let the water out and helped her step out of the tub. He patted her dry and wrung out her hair before combing through it. "You're a goddess," he told her as he set the comb down.

"I guess that makes you a god." She turned in his arms, grabbed the hem of his shirt, and pulled it over his head. "You have more tattoos than you had then."

"Yeah."

She ran her fingers over them, examining his chest and arms.

He held his breath as she lowered her gaze to the tattoo under his pec. "What's this one?"

He bit his lip and stared at the top of her head. Maybe he should lie. Make something up. But he couldn't lie to her. Not ever.

She lifted her gaze. "Rock? It looks like a sketchbook."

He nodded. "It is."

She leaned closer and spread her fingers around the tattoo, getting a better view. "Jesus, Rock. Oh my God."

He pursed his lips.

"My name is in this. You tattooed my name on your body. When did you do this?"

He drew in a breath. "That summer."

She set her forehead against his pecs, breathing heavily before kissing the tattoo. "I can't… Did anyone ever know? The letters are so subtle."

"No. No one ever knew." He understood what she'd meant. Had his wife known?

She had not. He'd told her the tattoo was from an art phase. He hadn't wanted to hurt her. There had been no need. When he'd been with Kathy, she'd been his world. He had never cheated on her, not even emotionally. He'd loved her. Their love hadn't been like the love he felt for Lyla. It had been different, but he'd loved her and mourned deeply when she'd left them.

Lyla moved her hands to the button on his jeans and popped it open, lowering the zipper moments later.

He didn't move or deny her whatever she needed. He simply stroked her hair while she lowered his jeans over his hips, taking his briefs with them.

His cock popped free, and he tried to focus on anything else in the world to keep from coming without her touching him. It had been so fucking long since he'd been with a woman, and this wasn't some random woman. This was his

Little Lyla. His Little girl. His world. For the rest of his days, he would worship her in every way she would let him.

He suddenly realized he didn't care if she never wanted to hone her Little side. It would change nothing. He loved her so deeply that he would do anything for her, including tamping down the Daddy side of him that wanted to push to the surface. If Lyla couldn't do it, he would never pressure her. He would love her until they died wrapped in each other's arms. Age play be damned.

Lyla abandoned his jeans when they were around his knees and reached up to stroke his cock. "I remember this," she murmured.

He chuckled lightly and reached down to stroke a finger over her nipple. "I remember this."

"You changed my life that night," she said reverently. "You ruined me."

He shuddered and grabbed the edge of the vanity. "That was my goal," he admitted.

"I never had sex like that again. I told myself it was a fluke." She tipped her head back. "You made me come."

He sucked in a breath. Had no one else ever made her come? "Baby…" He cupped her face.

"I need you inside me. I need your mouth on me. I need…" She dropped her gaze, grabbed his hips, and wrapped her lips around his cock.

He moaned and arched forward, gripping the vanity hard. *Jesus, fuck.*

She sucked him in deep, moaning around his shaft. His knees threatened to buckle. "Lyla…"

He grabbed her shoulders. "Baby girl, you have to stop. I'm going to come."

She shook him off and gripped the base of his cock with one small hand, bobbing up and down, driving him out of his mind in seconds. He couldn't stop her. He didn't have the energy. He'd already told her he was going to come. Obviously, that wasn't a deterrent.

His balls drew up, and he tipped his head back before he finally stopped fighting the need and screamed out his release.

Lyla swallowed every drop, moaning around his shaft. When he was fully spent, she finally released him with a pop and looked up at him. "That was so hot."

He groaned. "Baby girl, that's my line."

She rose to her feet. "Maybe we should move to the bed?"

CHAPTER
SIXTEEN

Lyla watched as Rock removed the rest of his clothes and dropped them in the hamper. Her breath hitched as she got her first look at his totally naked body.

Damn, he was sexy. They were both older, but Rock looked even sexier now than he had four decades ago. He was fit and ripped. She knew he'd had a heart attack, but apparently he'd taken damn fine care of himself since then.

He grabbed her around the waist and backed her out of the bathroom and into the bedroom. "We're going to need a bigger house," he muttered.

"Why?" She liked his house. It was cozy and welcoming. What more did they need?

Holy hell, why was she thinking as though she was definitely staying? She was in a dream. Nothing seemed real. Maybe none of this had happened and she was still sleeping at the motel on the night she'd arrived, wishful thinking filling her head.

"I don't like the look on your face, Baby girl," Rock growled as the back of her legs hit the mattress. He cupped her face. "What's going on in your pretty head, Little Lyla?"

She threaded her fingers in his hair at the back of his head.

It was gray, but it was still thick and soft. "I'm struggling to believe this is real," she whispered.

He kissed her. "It's real." He kissed her again, this time behind her ear. "This is also real." He lowered his head to kiss one of her nipples. "And this."

Her breath hitched when he lifted her by the hips and sat her on the bed, encouraging her to lie back. He grabbed her knees, pushed her legs open, and bent to kiss her pussy. "And this… Mmmm… This is very fucking real."

She fisted the sheets at her sides, arching her chest and moaning when he lowered his face again and sucked her clit.

Yes. Oh, God, yes. This… She remembered this. It had not changed. The fireworks between them were just as real as they had been when she'd been eighteen.

Over the years, she'd decided she'd surely embellished their hours together. That night couldn't have been as amazing as she remembered it. But now… Now that his mouth was on her again, she realized, if anything, she'd downplayed their time together.

He thrust his tongue into her channel and then lapped at her clit, holding her legs wide the entire time.

She stopped breathing, unable to focus on anything but the feel of his lips on her skin, the way he grazed his teeth lightly over her clit, his thumbs holding her pussy open, his breath hitting her sensitive parts, his nose nuzzling her, the purring sound coming from him vibrating through her body.

Suddenly, he released one of her legs and thrust a finger into her. "Fuck, you're tight, Little Lyla. Come, Baby girl. Come on Daddy's finger. I want to feel your cunt clench around me."

His words were so dirty that she couldn't stop herself. Her orgasm rushed to the surface, taking over her body and sending waves of pulses to her pussy.

"That's my girl. Jesus, you're sexy. I've never forgotten the look on your face when you came for me the first time.

Heavenly. I want to see that every day for the rest of my life."

She was panting as he scooted her back and climbed over her. He hovered on his knees between her legs, his hands on either side of her head. He looked down at her, his expression serious, his brow intense, his eyes wandering around her face. "You're mine."

She nodded.

"Say it, Little Lyla. Say that you're mine."

She licked her lips. "I'm yours, Rock." She reached for him, needing him to touch her. She wanted to feel him pressed against her body.

When he settled over her with his cock at her entrance, she wrapped her legs around him.

"I need you, Rock. Please. Hard and fast. I want to feel you filling me."

"Condom?" he asked.

She laughed. "No." She schooled her face a moment later as a memory assaulted her. "Unless you've been with ten other women lately."

He frowned. "No. I haven't been with anyone since long before my heart attack."

"It's been longer than that for me." She stroked his back. She believed him. She had no reason not to.

"So, bare?" he asked.

"I'm not going to get pregnant, if that's a concern." She gave him a sly grin.

He chuckled. "I wouldn't give a fuck if you did." Less than a second after those words left his mouth, he thrust all the way in, taking her breath away.

The sound that came out of her mouth was foreign to her. She hadn't felt this good in… Not since she'd been with him. It was pitiful but true.

He eased out and thrust back in, deeper, scrambling her brain.

She gripped his back with her fingertips.

He lowered his head and sucked one of her nipples into his mouth.

She moaned again, louder. Thank goodness he didn't have neighbors close by.

Rock switched to the other nipple, tormenting it with his tongue and teeth while he slid in and out of her.

Lyla felt alive. More alive than she had in years. The only time she'd ever felt like this had been that night they'd spent together. It hadn't been a fluke. It was Rock. It was *them*.

She lifted her hips, meeting him thrust for thrust. She hoped whatever issues he'd had with his heart weren't serious enough that he shouldn't be doing this. She should have asked more questions about his health.

Rock released her nipple and met her gaze as he slid a hand between them and found her clit. "Come on my cock, Little Lyla. Remind me what it feels like to have your cunt strangling me."

When he pinched her clit, she cried out, milking him with her pussy. The orgasm was more powerful than the one he'd given her with his mouth. The intensity took her by surprise. The waves of pleasure went on and on for longer than she'd ever experienced.

At some point in the middle of her blissed-out state, Rock emptied himself into her. He groaned loudly as the pulses of his release shook them.

She focused on his face as soon as she was able and found him smiling absently, his eyes on hers. She wrapped her arms around him and pulled him down. "I want your weight on me. All of it."

"Baby girl, I'm too heavy."

She shook her head. "No, you're not. I need to feel the pressure. Please."

He dropped lower, resting his chest against hers, his cock still lodged inside her.

She sighed and danced her fingers up and down his spine. "There are no words," she whispered.

"There are so many words," he responded, "but I can't put them into coherent sentences."

She giggled. "Okay, maybe that."

He eventually eased out. "Don't move. I'll be right back."

She watched as he padded from the room, breathing heavily. Could she really have this?

A minute later, he returned with a wet washcloth. He spread her legs gently and cleaned her up.

She shivered from the sweat on her skin and the cool air in the room.

He climbed into bed, pulled the covers over them, and dropped onto his back.

She snuggled into his side, wrapping her leg over his, hugging his chest. "Tell me about your heart," she whispered as she played with the hair on his pecs.

"They put a stent in. My heart is probably in better shape than ever because Remi has been forcing healthy food down my throat and making sure I exercise."

"Good. I'll do the same."

They lay there in comfortable silence for a long time while Lyla's mind ran in ten-thousand directions. She pictured her condo in Florida. It meant nothing to her. It was just a place to sleep. Did her parents really need her close by? No. She'd only moved there because why not?

But this was happening so fast. "Are we being reckless?" she asked softly.

He tipped his head down to look at her. "No." He didn't hesitate.

She rose onto her elbow to face him more directly. "We barely know each other. It's been so long. We're jumping in so fast." The truth was she was scared out of her mind. If she lost him again…

"We know everything that matters, Baby girl. We know we

still have the same chemistry we had back then. We know how we feel when we're together. We'll figure the rest out one day at a time. We'll learn each other's likes and dislikes as we go along."

She swallowed. He had an answer for everything. "You're so confident. Maybe we should take a step back and not rush."

He cupped her face. "Baby girl, if you think I'll let you walk out that door when I just got you back, you are sadly mistaken."

His intensity was undeniable. He was serious. He wasn't going to let her go. That meant a lot to her.

He brought her face closer to his. "I mean it, Lyla. I'll cuff you to the bed if I think you might slip away in the night."

She drew in a deep breath. "I won't slip away." She dropped back down alongside him, snuggling into his warmth, wrapped so tightly to his side that there wasn't a millimeter of space between them anywhere.

He stroked her arm up and down while they lay in the peaceful quiet for a while. Finally, he spoke. "Will you tell me why you never came back?"

She inhaled slowly and nodded. Over the past day, she'd begun to wonder if the information she'd had about him back then hadn't been accurate. She'd never questioned it before, but something felt off about it now.

"Were you seeing other women at that time?" she asked.

He flinched and then extricated himself from beneath her, rolled her to her back, and hovered over her. "Seeing other women?"

She nodded, gritting her teeth.

He searched her face. "Lyla, I didn't go on a single date with a single woman from the day I met you until long after you left."

She gasped. "Seriously?" Her voice squeaked. Was he telling the truth?

He frowned. "You stole my heart the first time I saw you. I

had no interest in anyone else. It was all I could do to keep my fucking jeans on every time I came to your house. I was a nutjob. While my friends were off sowing their fucking wild oats, I was pining for a girl who wasn't old enough to touch. Where the hell is this coming from?"

She swallowed. "Jackson… He said…"

Rock's eyebrows shot to the ceiling, his body went rigid, and then he groaned. He flattened one hand on his face and stroked it down to his beard. "Fuck." He sat upright, rubbing his chin. "*Fuck.*"

She waited for him to say something else. She couldn't tell if it was him or Jackson who'd lied to her. All she could do was wait for him to elaborate. *Fuck* wasn't quite enough information.

His eyes grew watery, and she thought he might cry. His face was tight as he looked away from her, sitting more fully. Finally, his body slumped. "I did this. It's my fault. Why the fuck did it never occur to me?"

She sat up and moved behind him. Something was terribly out of whack here, but she felt drawn to him anyway. She wrapped her arms around his neck from behind and flattened her chest to his back. She kissed his shoulder. "Tell me."

He groaned. "I'm an idiot."

"No, you're not."

He chuckled, but there was no humor in it. "Oh, yeah. I really am." He suddenly spun around, grabbed her, and hauled her to his front so that she straddled him. His hands came to her waist, holding her in place.

She stroked his shoulders, waiting for more.

He took a deep breath. "I constantly worried that your brother would figure out I was in love with you. It scared me to death. I was afraid that if he found out, he would punch me in the face and tell me to get lost. Then I wouldn't get to see you at all. I didn't want anything to rock the precarious boat I was floating in. I wanted free rein to come and go from your house, see you every day."

She nodded. He needed to elaborate. She still didn't know where this was going.

"So I often told Jackson I had a date. I let him believe that I was with various women when I wasn't with him. He didn't ask who they were because I pretended they were with the MC. It was a precarious game I played so that he wouldn't figure out the woman I really wanted was you."

Her entire body stiffened as she sat up straighter. Suddenly, it all made sense.

Rock groaned. "Fuck. I guess he told you I was a player."

She nodded, fighting back tears. He was fighting his own. They were staring at each other through two sets of glassy eyes. She licked her lips. "It was after that night. I was mopey when you left town for your internship. I didn't want Jackson to know we'd been together, but I wanted to know anything I could about you, so I asked him if he'd heard from you as nonchalantly as possible. He chuckled and shrugged. 'Nope. He's probably busy with one of the sweetbutts.' I didn't have a clue what a sweetbutt was at the time, so I asked. Jackson told me it was a term for women who hang around the club. Various women you were probably sleeping with." She let her voice trail off.

Rock gripped her firmly and set his forehead against hers. "He didn't lie to you. I told him all of that, but it never occurred to me he would end up telling you about my fake sex life."

She scooted closer to Rock, nestling her pussy against his shaft. "I'm sorry," she murmured. "Sorry for so many reasons."

"Me, too, Baby girl. So very fucking sorry. I'll never forgive myself for letting you go like that."

"You have to," she told him. "You have to be able to put it behind you, or we can't move on. I don't want us constantly looking at each other with sad puppy eyes because of what we didn't have. We have to embrace the future and hold on to what we do have."

He gave her a small smile. "Why are you so wise?"

She shrugged. "Years of practice."

"We could have been together all those years."

She leaned back and held his gaze. "Would you give up Atlas, Remi, and Kathy if you could?"

He winced. "No."

She stared at him. "Then we have to assume Fate had a different plan for us. We're walking our path now. I'm here now. The timing must be exactly right. Fate put me here to close on my parents' house so I would run into you."

He grabbed her hips, rose, and spun around so fast her head was spinning by the time he lowered her to her back. Her legs and arms were still wrapped around him.

He stared deep into her eyes. "You're mine for the rest of our days. And we're going to make up for lost time by fucking like teenagers four times a day until we die."

She giggled. "Okay."

He kissed her. "Not another word about leaving or stepping back, got it?"

She nodded. "There are other considerations, you know. Namely that I'm not sure how Little I can be."

"I don't give a fuck about anything but how I feel when you're in my arms. I don't even want to leave you to go pee. The rest will work itself out."

"Okay…" She eased her fingers into his hair. "Maybe you could fuck me again while we're figuring it out."

He gave her a sexy grin while he rubbed his cock up and down her folds. He glanced at the clock. "Shit."

She stiffened. "What's wrong?"

"It's already nine. We only have three more hours to get two more rounds in."

She giggled. "I bet we can do it."

CHAPTER
SEVENTEEN

Rock couldn't take his gaze off his woman. It was so bad that he'd hoisted her onto the counter and made her sit there while he cooked breakfast. That way, he could keep her constantly in his peripheral vision while he flipped pancakes.

He'd set a box on the counter next to her, and now he nodded toward it. "Open it." It was a cardboard box with the flaps folded over. It didn't appear to be anything special.

She furrowed her brows. "What's in it?"

"Things I borrowed from the supply closet at the clubhouse yesterday. I put it in the car last night while you were on your tour with the Littles."

She eyed him suspiciously with one brow raised.

He chuckled. "Open it. Dig around."

"Okay…" She was trembling as she popped the box open and leaned over to peer at the contents. "Oh… Little things."

"Yep." He didn't say anything else. He didn't want to influence her. She had to come to grips with how Little she was on her own.

She started pulling things out, one at a time. "Sippy cup."

She giggled. "Every one of the women…girls…Littles…last night was using one of these."

"It's common." He glanced at her as he flipped the bacon.

"They had matching plates and sporks and stuff, too."

He nodded toward the box.

She reached in and pulled out a place setting, rolling her pretty eyes.

He chuckled. "Those eyes… You know some Daddies do not let their Little girls roll their eyes."

"Is that so?" Her face was so cute, all scrunched up and sassy. "Apparently, Kade doesn't let Remi do so."

"Nope. He does not."

"I suspect Remi does it often anyway."

"Yep." Rock felt lighter than he had in years. This banter was fun.

"So, after observing everyone last night, I'd say it's all a big game. There're all these rules in place about running and sassing and touching hot surfaces, and the girls spend most of their time intentionally breaking the rules so they can get their butts spanked."

"Basically, except it's more than a game. It's a lifestyle."

"But they go to work and out in public in an adult head-space, and they reserve their age play for when they're in the clubhouse."

"Or their own homes," Rock added. He pulled out the last of the bacon and poured the whipped eggs into the pan.

Lyla leaned toward him. "What do I have to do to get you to spank me?" she murmured in a sultry voice.

He nearly dropped the spatula. The eggs were done, so he turned off the burner and moved in front of her, grabbing her hips. "Baby girl, all you have to do is ask. If you like the idea of misbehaving to earn a spanking, that's fine. But if you don't care for that aspect, and you still want me to swat your bottom, just ask."

She set her hands on his shoulders. "You spanked me once before. I still remember it."

He grabbed one of her hands and brought her palm to his mouth to kiss it. "I do, too, like it was yesterday."

"I liked it."

"I know you did." Fuck, she was so adorable.

She chewed on her bottom lip, thinking before she released it. "It makes sense. I mean, if someone's under a lot of stress, it makes sense that a spanking would chase some of that away."

"Yes. Some Littles like to be spanked until they cry. Some prefer light swats that remind them they are loved."

"Am I?" she asked so softly he almost didn't hear her.

He wasn't sure what she meant for a moment, and then he knew. His heart got caught in his throat. "You are so loved, Little Lyla. I love you so much it hurts."

Her cheeks turned pink. "It's only been like a day."

"It's been forty years."

Her chest rose and fell with every deep breath. "I love you, too." She leaned forward and set her forehead against his. "Maybe we could skip breakfast and work on round two."

He chuckled. Perhaps he shouldn't have suggested they have sex four times a day. She was going to wear him out. And he was going to love every minute of it.

They'd managed to squeeze in three rounds last night before they passed out in each other's arms, but the last thing Lyla had muttered was that they'd have to go five rounds today to make up for it.

He'd stared at her with a huge grin on his face after she'd fallen asleep. And he'd woken up to her under the covers kissing his cock. It was mid-morning now that they were finally in the kitchen.

He shook his head. "Naughty girl. First, I'm going to feed you. Then I'm going to spank you so you can stop wondering what it will feel like. Then I'll fuck you until you scream. And then we'll go over to the house, check on the progress, and touch base with your brother."

Her eyes widened. "Oh, shit. Jackson. I forgot he was even here."

Rock chuckled. "I didn't. I texted him this morning and told him we would be there by noon. He's supervising."

She blew out a breath. "Oh, good." She twisted to the side, lifted the pink plastic plate from the counter, and handed it to him. "Feed me."

Two of the sweetest words in the English language.

Rock lifted her off the counter and guided her toward the table. He pulled out a chair. "Sit. I have an idea."

She slowly lowered her bottom to the seat, pulling the hem of his T-shirt under her.

He tipped her chin back. "Don't move, Little girl. I'll be right back." He headed for the bedroom. His idea might backfire on him, but his instinct told him it wouldn't.

When he returned, she was right where he'd left her.

Her eyes went wide when she saw what he was carrying.

Rock set the rope on the table and reached for the sides of her T-shirt. "Arms up."

Her breath hitched as she let him pull the shirt over her head, leaving her in nothing but cute bikini panties. Fuck, she was smoking hot. Every inch of her. She did not look fifty-six. Time had been kind to her.

Rock grabbed the rope and rounded behind her. "Reach your arms behind the chair, Little Lyla."

She did as he instructed, twisting her neck to look. "What are you going to do?"

"What do you think I'm going to do?"

She sighed and sat still while he carefully restrained one wrist and then the other, wrapping the rope up her arms. They couldn't come together, of course, but restraining her up to her elbows forced her to sit taller and thrust her chest forward.

Rock came to her front next and grabbed one end of the

rope to trap her ankle on the outside of the chair leg. He used the other end of the rope to secure her other ankle.

She was panting when he finished. "Rock…"

He sat in a chair next to hers and dragged her chair so that they were knees to knees. "Is the rope too tight anywhere, Baby girl?"

"No, Sir," she whimpered.

Fuck me. The way she said *Sir*…

Rock cupped her breasts gently and flicked his thumbs over her nipples.

She moaned and tipped her head back.

"My girl likes a bit of bondage."

"I don't think that was ever in question," she responded.

He headed for the stove and dished up eggs, bacon, and pancakes, putting hers on the pink plastic plate. He filled the sippy cup with apple juice.

She was panting harder when he returned. "Are you going to feed me?"

"Yes, Baby girl. I'm going to feed you."

"When I said *feed me*, I didn't mean it literally."

He chuckled. "You'll be more careful with your word choice next time, then."

She squirmed. "Rock…"

He set her plate down and stroked a finger over the soaked gusset of her panties, making her moan again.

"Rock!"

"I think I like having you tied down." He held the sippy cup up to her lips. "Take a drink, Little Lyla."

She twisted her head to one side and pursed her lips.

He chuckled. "Do you have any idea how Little you're being right now?"

She narrowed her gaze and glared at him. It wasn't in earnest, though. She was clearly fighting a grin.

He lifted her rubber spork and scooped up a bite of eggs. "Eating meals is a hard rule for Little girls. You'll eat until I'm satisfied you've had enough. Then I'll untie you and spank your bottom until it's bright red. I want you to remember it for several hours."

Her cheeks turned pink.

He leaned closer to her. "Yes, Daddy."

She licked her pretty lips. "Yes, Daddy."

"Good girl." His heart soared. He might be using a bit of coercion to get her to play along, but he suspected submitting to him wasn't something she was opposed to. She was just out of practice and needed some encouragement.

He lifted the bite to her lips, and his cock grew hard enough to bulge out of the top of his shorts when she opened for him and accepted the bite.

He stroked a finger under her chin. "Such a good girl." This time, when he offered her a drink from the sippy cup, she accepted it.

In between feeding her bites, he ate everything on his plate.

Lyla managed to eat a good amount of food, considering the fact that she was so horny she couldn't sit still. Rock loved every whimper and moan, every time she arched her chest or contracted her thighs. He loved how she lost her mind when he stroked her clit through the cotton of her panties or pinched her nipples.

"Are you full, Little Lyla?" he asked when he thought she'd had enough.

She nodded. "Yes...Daddy."

The word wasn't coming naturally to her yet, but it was still musical.

He left her sitting there while he cleaned the kitchen and wiped her face. He wanted her to simmer for a bit, think about how it felt to be restrained and at his mercy.

"Ready for your spanking, Baby girl?" he asked as he squatted down to untie her legs.

"Yes, Daddy." Her eyes were glazed with lust. She kept licking her lips. She wasn't arguing with him anymore.

Rock circled behind her to release her arms next, but as soon as she was free, he instructed, "Stand. Hands behind your back."

She obeyed him like the Little angel she was, and he retied her wrists at the small of her back before guiding her into the bedroom. He lifted her off her feet and set her on her knees.

Her lips were parted. "Daddy…"

He grabbed two pillows and set them in front of her. "I'm going to lower you over the pillows so that your bottom is in the air and your hands are trapped."

She whimpered as he helped her get into the position.

"Turn your face this way so I can see your expression at all times."

She did as she was told.

He stroked her cheek and tucked her hair behind her ear. "I'm going to spank you because it will feel good, not because you're in trouble. Afterward, I'm going to stroke your pussy until you come."

She shuddered and finally smiled. "Yes, Daddy."

He chuckled. That part she was into. He eased her panties down her legs. "Spread your knees wide, Little Lyla. I want to see your pussy glistening the entire time."

When she parted her thighs, he swatted her bottom hard. "More, naughty girl."

She cried out and spread them farther.

"That's better." The position was obscene and so fucking sexy. Her pussy was dripping from their foreplay at breakfast.

Rock rubbed her bottom where he'd just swatted it. "Does it sting?"

"Yes, Daddy."

"You want more, though, don't you?"

"Yes, Daddy."

"Good girl. I'm going to start slowly, but I'm not going to go easy on you. I want you to really let go of your stress. Everything feels like it's upside down in your life, and I get that. But I want you to learn to trust me to know what you need and take care of you. Do you understand?"

"Yes, Daddy."

"Did you like being tied to the chair while I fed you, Little Lyla?" He rubbed her bottom and the backs of her thighs, letting his fingers come precariously close to her pussy over and over.

She lifted her head. "Yes, Daddy."

"It felt good to give up that control, didn't it?" He tapped her pussy.

She arched her body, lifting her head higher. Her voice was high-pitched when she cried out, "Yes, Daddy."

"Good girl." He waited for her to rest her cheek back on the mattress and then lifted his palm to swat her fantastic bottom.

She moaned at the first contact.

His cock was harder than ever as he spanked her pretty bottom again, watching her reaction and nearly groaning at how deeply she was submitting to him. Instead of tensing like most people would for their first spanking, she relaxed into the pillows.

This wasn't exactly her first spanking, but it had been a fucking long time. She shouldn't remember it so well. But that wasn't what she needed to remember. What Lyla knew in her soul that hadn't ever left her was that she trusted Rock. It was evident in everything she did. She trusted him, and it humbled him to the core.

He continued to spank her until her bottom was hot and red. Instead of fighting him, she was totally into it, lifting her bottom to ask for more. When she started to close her thighs once, he swatted the insides of her legs.

She didn't do that again.

He waited for a deep shudder to wrack her body before he stopped.

She was panting, and her eyes were glazed. "Daddy..."

He set one hand on top of hers at the small of her back and reached between her thighs with the other.

She screamed when he stroked through her folds. Fuck, he loved that sound.

"That's my girl." He pushed two fingers into her, still stunned by how tight she was. "Come on Daddy's fingers."

That was all it took. She was so close to orgasm from the spanking alone that she cried out and arched her head off the bed as her entire body shook with her release.

While he continued to thrust in and out of her through the waves of her orgasm, he tugged the ends of the rope to free her hands. Finally, he climbed up between her legs, lifted her bottom into the air, and lined his cock up with her entrance. "Do you want Daddy's cock, Little Lyla?"

"God, yes. Please, Daddy." She rose onto her elbows.

He grabbed her hips and thrust in to the hilt.

Lyla keened, the sound animalistic as it vibrated through the house. It was enough to bring him right to the edge. He came after only a few strokes. It wasn't difficult to believe after nearly an hour of foreplay. His cock had been hard from the moment he'd tied her to the kitchen chair.

When they were both spent, he eased their connected bodies to one side and spooned her with his erection still firmly inside her warmth. He stroked her everywhere. "I love you, Lyla."

"I love you, too, Rock."

He closed his eyes and luxuriated in this new life development. Heaven. It was the only word he could come up with. He could spend days or weeks or months kicking himself for all the time they'd lost because of his stupidity, but it wouldn't change anything. They had a lot of years left, and he intended to spend them with his girl. Every minute of every hour of every day.

She was a precious gift. He'd been given a second chance.

He would not squander it. Live life to the fullest. He held her close, and she gripped his hand between her breasts.

"So, maybe I'm a tiny bit Little," she murmured.

He chuckled, shaking both of them. "Just a bit." He kissed her shoulder. "Now, we need a shower so we don't smell like sex when we go meet your brother."

She groaned and gripped his hand tighter as if she could keep him from moving. "I'm comfy."

"Sassy girl. You're already mastering the whiny aspect of age play."

She giggled. "I'm not sure I can embrace all of it, but I bet I can role-play often when we're alone. Will that be enough for you?"

"There is nothing you can do that won't be enough for me, Little Lyla. You're my heart. You don't have to be Little at all to please me." He hadn't believed that was possible two days ago. In fact, he'd told her being a Daddy was in his soul. And maybe it was, but his feelings for her were so much bigger. He'd hang the moon for her. He'd also give her exactly what she needed from age play or any other kink. And he'd do so with all the love in the world filling his heart.

CHAPTER
EIGHTEEN

"I feel naughty," Lyla whispered as soon as they stepped out of the car at her parents' house.

He chuckled as he pulled her into his arms. "Because I fucked you clear into tomorrow? Or because your bottom is so hot you can't sit down? Or…" He slid a hand up her back and snapped her bra, "…is it because under this adult sweater and jeans, you're wearing a frilly pink bra and panties?"

Her face heated. "All of the above." She swatted at him, trying not to let him embarrass her. "Stop making me horny. My brother is going to know we fucked."

"Baby girl, if your brother doesn't know we're fucking after the kiss you planted on me yesterday, he's an idiot."

She grinned and shrugged. "You're right. Why do I care?"

He lowered his hand to squeeze her butt cheek, making her jump and squeal. He gave her a swat. "What's wrong, Little Lyla? Does the elastic from those naughty Little girl panties hurt your hot bottom?"

She narrowed her gaze at him. "Behave."

He chuckled and took her hand. "Baby girl, I don't care who sees us or what anyone thinks. I'm willing to climb onto the roof and scream at the top of my lungs that Lyla Sealock is my woman. I want the entire world to know. No way am I going to hide my feelings."

She cupped his face and kissed him. The neighbors were probably watching, but she didn't care. She took his hand as they headed toward the house.

When they stepped inside, Lyla was surprised to see Jackson with work clothes on and a paint roller in his hands. He looked up and chuckled. "About time you two got here. Sheesh." He was teasing.

He looked back and forth between the two of them, grinning. "I still can't believe I never knew the two of you…"

Rock shook his head. "There was never anything going on between us before your sister turned eighteen." He lifted a finger. "And, for the record, I was not some manwhore sleeping around with everyone in a skirt. I lied about that so you wouldn't know I was into your sister."

Jackson's eyes went wide. "Seriously?"

"Yes."

The paint roller slid out of Jackson's hand and hit the floor. Luckily, it hadn't been dipped in paint yet. He ran a hand through his hair. "But…"

Lyla felt bad for him. She knew he would beat himself up over this if she didn't stop it. "It wasn't your fault."

Rock shook his head. "It was definitely *my* fault."

Lyla twisted to look at Rock. "Maybe it was *my* fault. Huh?" Her voice rose. "I'm the one who believed that shit about you as if I didn't know better. I'm the one who didn't come to you and ask if it was true."

Rock reached out for her and pulled her into his arms. He kissed the top of her head. "Okay, Baby girl. Let's stop placing blame. It's done. No more blaming. We can't undo what happened. We're here now."

He tipped her head back and forced her to meet his gaze.

She swallowed and fought back another round of tears.

"What did we say this morning, huh? We said we weren't

going to waste time lamenting the past. We're moving forward. Every day is ours from now on. All of them. Hundreds of days. Thousands. We won't squander them."

She nodded hard. He was right. They were together now.

"Wow, you two really are in love, aren't you?" Jackson asked softly. "How stupid am I that I never noticed?"

Rock tucked Lyla under his arm. "We were self-absorbed young people back then. Enough. We're done discussing the past."

Lyla fisted his shirt in her palm and plastered herself to his side.

A knock sounded at the open door, and Lyla turned around to see the two officers from the other night.

"May we come in?" Susan asked.

"Of course." Rock released Lyla to hurry over and open the door wider.

Lyla wrung her hands in front of her. She prayed they had some information. She was going to look over her shoulder every time she left the house until they caught the man who'd attacked her.

Susan didn't look happy, though. "We spoke to the previous renters—the Housemans. They're in an assisted living facility just outside of town now. They said they haven't seen or heard from their son in a few months, but he had been to the house a few times before that. He did occasionally sleep in that room upstairs where you suspected he was stashing something. The Housemans believe he was doing drugs. It could have been drugs. It could have been money. It could have been both."

"So no one knows where he is?" Jackson asked.

Susan glanced at him.

Jackson stepped forward and held out a hand. "I'm sorry. I'm Jackson Sealock, Lyla's brother. I arrived yesterday. I'm getting caught up."

Susan nodded. "I'm sorry we don't have more information.

It's best you remain diligent until we locate him. If he believes you have something of his, he's probably not going to let it go until he gets it back."

Lyla rubbed her temples. "It's madness. I don't have anything."

"We know that, but he doesn't," Susan pointed out.

Rock wrapped an arm around Lyla's middle again. "He can't hide forever. Someone will find him."

"We'll be in touch," Susan said before the two officers left.

Jackson turned toward Lyla and Rock. "If it's Carl, and he's watching the place, he surely knows you've been coming and going together. He might follow you."

Rock sighed. "You're right. We'll stay at the clubhouse tonight. No one can get in there."

Jackson bent to pick up the paint roller. "I decided the house would sell faster if it had a fresh coat of paint."

"We'll help," Rock stated.

"A few of your guys are downstairs. They finished the drywall, and they're painting now. I figured I'd start up here. No reason to worry about the carpet. We'll have it pulled out next. I say we just tape the trim and give this place a fresh coat of off-white."

Lyla glanced at Rock. She wasn't sure painting was something he was up to, but he clapped his hands together and said, "I'll grab some old shirts from the back of my car."

CHAPTER
NINETEEN

I t was dinnertime when Rock led his girl into the clubhouse. Everyone who was there this evening was at the giant table, talking and laughing and stuffing their faces.

They looked up when he entered with Lyla.

Steele grinned. "Hey. Grab some plates. Bear has outdone himself tonight."

"Thanks." Rock guided Lyla toward the kitchen sink, pinned her in, and turned on the water. He set his lips on her ear. "Give me your hands, Baby girl."

Her breath hitched as he washed their combined hands. He loved that sound and the way she started breathing heavily.

"You okay with this?" he whispered.

She nodded. "I'm good. Starving. It smells delicious."

"I'm sure it is." He grabbed a few paper towels and dried their combined hands next. He didn't ask her what sort of plate she wanted. Now wasn't the time to push her to let her Little out. She might never be comfortable being Little in front of others. That was okay.

He grabbed two regular plates and nodded toward the counter where all the food was spread out. The members often filled their plates at the counter and then joined everyone at the table. It was more efficient than passing dishes around.

"Oh, God. Fried chicken," Lyla murmured. "That looks so good."

Rock filled her plate, glancing up to make sure he was choosing things she would want. She didn't even flinch. She let him add mashed potatoes, gravy, green beans, and a roll.

Maybe plastic plates and youthful dresses would never be her thing in front of others, but Rock wasn't unaware that he was Daddying her in many ways anyway. Filling her plate, pulling out her chair, pushing her up to the table, setting a napkin in her lap, getting her a drink... All of that filled his heart. He wanted to take care of her. That was the most important thing, no matter what it looked like.

She smiled at him as he sat next to her. "Thank you." She leaned into him and kissed his cheek. "It feels nice to have someone dote on me."

"I'll dote on you for the rest of our lives, Little Lyla."

After dinner, Rock helped some of the other men clean up while Remi and Carlee took Lyla to the library off the common room. It was filled with games and books. It was also where the Littles most often cooked up their shenanigans.

Rock forced himself not to panic. Lyla was a grown woman. She could handle herself. She wasn't judgmental, so he knew she wouldn't flinch over the level of age play Remi and Carlee practiced. Lyla was perfectly capable of setting her boundaries.

When the kitchen was clean, he made a beeline for the library but stopped when he saw Kade and Atlas standing outside the room.

Kade held a finger up to his lips.

Rock joined them as Atlas held a hand up to cup his ear, indicating they were spying on the girls.

Rock wasn't sure he liked eavesdropping on Lyla or anyone else, but as soon as he heard them talking, he relaxed.

At first, there was giggling, and then Lyla said, "So, let me get this straight, you two were childhood friends?"

"Yep." That voice was Carlee's. "I had the hots for Atlas, but he was way too old for me, and then he went away to college and didn't come back until recently."

"That's so sweet," Lyla said.

"Kinda like you and Dad," Remi added, "only Atlas wasn't gone nearly as long."

"Okay," Lyla continued, "back to the tree. I'm confused about it. There's a big tree out in the yard and you used to climb it? And it's still there?"

"Yep," Carlee said. "So, before I got together with Atlas, I was in an abusive relationship with a previous club member named Silver. He didn't like that I left him, and he eventually came here to the compound, hunting me down. I got scared and scrambled up into the tree to hide from him. I don't think Atlas has ever been more panicked."

Lyla's breath hitched loudly. "You must have been so scared."

"I thought Atlas would lose his mind," Remi agreed. "But the important thing is that we still climb that tree sometimes. We all played a trick on Dad one day and hid up there when he was supposed to be watching us."

Rock smiled and rubbed his chest. He loved that his woman was comfortable enough to join his daughter and his son's Little girl. It made him feel whole, like his family was a full unit.

The girls fell into a fit of giggles.

"I wish I had been there to see his face," Lyla said through laughter.

"Oh, don't you worry," Carlee told her. "Pulling stunts on our Daddies is a way of life here. We'll have you joining in our troublemaking in no time."

"So, you all plot these wild shenanigans, and then

everyone gets spanked?" Lyla asked, still giggling through all the words.

"Yep." Remi was laughing, too. "We would never drag you into anything you don't want to participate in, of course. We aren't mean. It's all in good fun. If you don't like to be naughty, that's okay. And, also, not every Little girl likes to be spanked. If that's not your thing, I'm sure you and Rock will come up with whatever discipline suits you."

"I don't think I have a problem with the spanking," Lyla admitted, "but I don't think I'd like Rock to spank me in front of other people. Do they do that?"

"Not if it's not something you enjoy," Carlee explained. "A lot of Littles don't like to be exposed in front of other people. Their Daddies dole out their punishments in their own apartments. A few like to be watched, so they get their panties pulled down right in the common room."

"But," Remi added, "only if everyone present doesn't mind watching that sort of thing. Consenting to being in a room where people are getting spanked is just as important as consenting to have your own bottom spanked."

"That's kind of nice," Lyla muttered.

"I'm so glad you're here," Remi said. "I'll let you know when we plan the next great stunt. You can decide if you want to join in."

Rock had to cover his mouth to keep from chuckling. Atlas and Kade were also stifling laughter. It was time to break up the huddle, though, before Lyla ended up in over her head. He didn't think she was ready to get corralled into whatever these girls might plot this evening.

Rock motioned toward Kade and Atlas so they would know he was planning to step into the room, and then he rounded the corner. He found Lyla sitting in a circle with Remi and Carlee, just as he'd expected. He narrowed his gaze at all of them. "Are you naughty girls plotting something?"

They all shook their heads, even Lyla.

Kade and Atlas joined him. Kade reached for Remi. "Time for bed, princess."

"You, too, Carlee," Atlas said.

As the girls stood, Rock pulled Lyla into his arms. He didn't know how many moments of sheer bliss he'd experienced today, but this was definitely one of them. Damn, he loved her.

CHAPTER
TWENTY

"So this is your apartment…" Lyla wandered around the set of rooms Rock apparently called home when he stayed at the clubhouse. It was really two rooms. The main room was sectioned off—his bedroom area was on one side and the living area was on the other, complete with a mini-fridge and a microwave. The second room was the attached bathroom.

"Yep. It's hardly smaller than my house."

She shrugged. "I like your house. It's cozy."

"It's a bachelor pad. It's tiny. We'll sell it and get something larger."

She might have panicked if he'd said something like that even ten hours ago, but she found she liked him including her in his future as if it were a done deal.

She came to him, wrapped her arms around his waist, and tipped her head back. "You're not selling your house. I like it just how it is."

He rubbed her arms, brows furrowed. "Baby girl, I wouldn't care if we shared a two-hundred-square-foot room for the rest of our lives. I like the thought of always having you in my sight and close enough that I can reach out and touch you or grab you and haul you onto my lap, but I bet you'll eventually like to have some space."

"Nope. I like you watching me. I like you snagging me when I pass you. All I need is some art supplies in a corner, and I'll be happy."

He nuzzled her neck. "When are you going to let me see your sketchbook? It's always in your satchel, but you haven't pulled it out much in the last few days."

"We've been kind of busy." She smoothed her hands on his firm chest. "I've never let anyone see it."

"*Never*? No one?"

She shook her head. "Nope. Not the sketchbooks. Other things, yes, but not that."

"Now, I'm even more intrigued."

"Mmm. Maybe someday."

Rock guided her toward the bed and began removing her clothes, starting with her shirt. "We need sleep."

"I think we're still two orgasms short for the day," she joked. She was pretty tired herself.

He chuckled. "You're making me younger by the hour." He took her hand and set her palm on his cock. It was fully erect.

She squeezed it through his jeans. "Take your shirt off. I want to see my name on your chest again. I still can't believe you tattooed my name on you."

He cupped her face and kissed her gently. "I wanted a piece of you with me forever. Even if I never saw you again, the time we had together was incredibly important to me. A monumental experience. I didn't want to forget it."

She sniffled. "I'm not going to cry."

"Don't. You're here now. *Mine*. Mine forever." He kissed her again before leaning back a few inches to haul his shirt over his chest and toss it on the floor where he'd thrown hers.

They silently undressed each other, taking their time, kissing each other's bodies all over until Rock pulled the covers back on the bed and motioned for her to climb in.

Lyla slid toward the center, sighing contentedly when Rock joined her. He pulled her against him, chest to chest. "You don't have any tattoos," he commented.

She shook her head. "Nope. Maybe I should get your name on my boob or something so we match."

He chuckled. "Not your forehead?"

She giggled as she slid her hand down to wrap it around his cock, loving the way he groaned as she circled the thick shaft and stroked up and down.

"You're going to kill me."

"I hope not. I have plans for you."

"Four times a day, apparently," he joked.

"Yep." She pushed him onto his back, climbed over him, and straddled his sexy body.

His breath hitched as she set her hands on his shoulders, leaning forward so that her breasts hung between them. Her pussy nestled against his length.

Rock cupped her breasts. "Fuck, you're sexy. I'm certain you're more gorgeous than you were at eighteen."

"I was thinking the same thing about you."

He set a hand on the small of her back and hauled her down until he could wrap his lips around her nipple.

She squealed when he nipped the bud, and then she bit her lip and glanced around.

"Don't worry, we were pretty thorough with insulation when we designed these rooms."

Still biting her bottom lip, she lifted her weight up a few inches, letting his cock rise until it lodged at her entrance. Holding his gaze, she slammed down onto him, all the way to the hilt.

Even though she'd known what was coming, she was unprepared for how good it felt to be filled with him yet again. Her eyes rolled back as she ground her pussy against the base of his cock. *Fuck...* So good.

Lyla tipped her head back and purred. She was so damn

glad she'd returned to Shadowridge. What if she'd gone the rest of her life wandering around with no real purpose or plan? That's what it had felt like for years. Suddenly, she felt grounded. Her roots were here. Not in Florida. Her life was in the apartment, or the house Rock owned, or any other place she was with him. It didn't matter where. It only mattered that his hands were on her and his eyes roamed her body.

She lowered her gaze to find him staring into her soul even now as she thought exactly that. The intensity in his eyes was so powerful and consuming. It made her feel like she was…home.

She eased up and down on his shaft slowly, torturing both of them, letting her breasts sway between their bodies. She never took her eyes off his as the need grew until he stiffened beneath her. His hips bucked upward. "Come, Little Lyla. Come with me."

She did, a dizzying experience she never wanted to end.

CHAPTER
TWENTY-ONE

Lyla took a sip of her coffee and looked over the rim at her brother.

Jackson had been smirking since they'd arrived at the coffee shop. "So...Rock."

She wasn't surprised this was what he led with. "Yep."

"I didn't think he was going to agree to let you leave his side to meet me this morning." He was still smirking, clearly half serious, half joking around.

"I can't really blame him. The last time I walked away from him, I was gone for thirty-eight years."

Jackson chuckled. "Okay. There is that. So... How did this all happen exactly?"

Lyla lifted a brow. "You want me to tell you about Rock and me from forty years ago?"

"I think so. Do I?"

"No. You don't." Lyla smiled at him. "Trust me. I can't even make it PG. Let's just say he was there when I needed him one night toward the end of my senior year, and we had a connection."

Jackson drew in a deep breath. "Okay. And you're...in love with him?"

"Yes."

"You've been here for three days."

"I was probably always in love with him, Jackson. He was my first love. Now he's my last love." She wanted Jackson's blessing, but it wasn't necessary. It wouldn't change anything.

"I always liked that guy," Jackson said.

She chuckled. "Me, too."

His face scrunched up. "How far back does this infatuation go? How the hell did I not notice?"

"I knew the day I met him. You wouldn't even remember that day because it wasn't consequential to you, but I remember it vividly. So does Rock. But you have to know neither of us acted on those feelings. He was extremely respectful of the fact that I was sixteen. We didn't even acknowledge our shared attraction. Not until after I was eighteen."

Jackson nodded slowly. "I'm not surprised. The guy didn't even smoke pot. It was always so comical that Mom and Dad thought he might be a bad influence on me. It was the other way around, though. Rock never wavered on his stance about illegal substances."

Lyla smiled. "He's a good guy."

"He's also smart as a whip. I never told anyone, but the reason I befriended him in the first place was because I needed his help with Calculus."

Lyla laughed. "Jackson... I'm not that naïve. Nor are Mom and Dad. We all knew that."

His brows shot up. "You did?"

"Of course."

"So, what are you going to do now? Stay here in town?"

"Yes." She didn't hesitate. There was no decision to be made.

"Mom and Dad will be sorry to see you leave Florida."

"Yeah, but they don't need me. Not really. Not yet anyway." She drew in a breath. In the back of her mind, she had some concerns that her parents would eventually need help. She wasn't sure how she would juggle that if she moved back to Shadowridge, but she'd cross that bridge if and when she came to it.

Jackson leaned forward and set his elbows on the table. "I was actually thinking about moving to Florida myself."

"You were?" She sat straighter and took another sip of her coffee.

"Yeah. I'm tired of the rat race in New York. My kids aren't even in the area anymore. I work from home most of the time. And it's fucking cold in the winter."

"Need a condo?" she joked.

He stared at her for a moment. "Maybe I do."

"I was kidding. Kind of. But if you want my condo, that would certainly be tidy."

"I could at least move into it in the short run. Then I wouldn't have to deal with also hunting for a place to live. I was really dreading that part. Would you leave your furniture? I was thinking of selling everything. It's not cost-effective to move furniture."

"Fuck, Jackson. I'll leave everything you want. You can't imagine how much weight that would lift off my shoulders. I could pick up my personal things and hand you the keys."

Jackson set his mug down and held out a hand. "I think we have a deal."

She laughed as she shook it as if they were strangers making a business arrangement.

Jackson sobered as he sat back. "I'm so pleased to see you this happy. It never really occurred to me that you weren't happy. But now that I see you alive and smiling, I realize you haven't been happy for years."

"Yeah, I didn't think about it much either. I think what happened was that I had this great thing, and it was so fleeting, and then it was over, and I never found that again. Nothing ever measured up. The moment Rock stepped back into my life the other night, everything fell into place as if no time had passed. Yes, we have a lot of life to talk about, but it's all just information. Details. It won't change how we feel about one another."

Jackson smiled. "I can see that, and I sincerely wish you all the best." He pushed his empty mug to the center of the table. "We should probably get back before Rock gets nervous and hunts us down. I think we'll have the painting finished later today. I have a carpet guy coming tomorrow. With all the extra help, we should have the house in great shape and on the market quickly."

Lyla took the last sip of her coffee and set the mug next to Jackson's. "Let me run to the bathroom really quick. That went right through me."

Jackson stood as she did. He looked around. "Do you know where it is?"

She turned and pointed. "Short hallway over there. I'll be right back."

"Rock will kill me if I lose sight of you."

She chuckled. "It's just the bathroom. You can watch the hallway the entire time. I'll be right back."

Lyla could laugh it off in front of Jackson, but she was putting up a front. She wasn't particularly excited about going to the bathroom alone either, but she needed to get over herself. It could be months before anyone found Carl. She couldn't spend her entire life in fear.

There was no one in the short hallway, and she entered the bathroom to find no one in there either. Two stalls. She was alone. She peed, washed her hands, and was just about to reach for the door when it suddenly opened.

It was not a woman. It was the same guy who had attacked her the other night. She assumed it was Carl, but she had no idea. She really didn't know what Carl looked like. Her mouth opened, instinct telling her to scream, but she wasn't fast enough. The man rushed into the room, grabbed her, slammed her against the wall, and covered her mouth.

Fear climbed up her spine as her eyes went wide. She couldn't breathe. He was pinching her nose. Panic made her struggle as much as possible, but he pinned her hard against the wall with his entire body.

His face was inches from hers when he hissed, "Where the fuck is my stuff, bitch?"

She shook her head as much as she could. She had no idea what the fuck stuff he was looking for. Money? Drugs? She didn't know.

He pulled out a knife and held it in front of her face. "Don't fuck with me, bitch."

She stiffened, eyes wider, fear making her vision blurry.

"If you make a sound, I will slit your throat. Do you understand, bitch?"

She gave a slight nod.

He lowered his hand to her throat. "Where is my fucking stuff?"

"I don't know what you're looking for. I swear. I don't know anything about your stuff."

He narrowed his gaze and leaned in closer, bringing the knife to her throat. His other hand was around her neck, pinning her almost too far off the floor. She was on her toes, trying not to choke.

"Don't fuck with me," he growled. "I'll cut you. You'll bleed out in this bathroom before anyone finds your body."

She drew in air through her nose, struggling on her toes. She brought one hand up to his arm and pushed against it. "I can't breathe," she managed to wheeze.

"I don't give a fuck if you breathe, bitch. Where's my shit?" The knife came too close to her and nicked her skin. She felt the warmth of blood running down her neck.

She considered telling him she had whatever he was looking for and would take him to it just to buy herself some time. But suddenly, the door flew open, slamming against the opposite wall. She expected to see Jackson or even some members of the MC, but she was relieved and surprised to see Rock.

In less than a second, he grabbed the back of her assailant and yanked him off her by the collar.

Lyla screamed as she scrambled a few inches toward the corner. She had nowhere to go. She flattened herself to the wall and grabbed her neck. She didn't think he'd cut her badly, but she wasn't certain.

Two men joined Rock and wrestled her attacker to the floor. One of them kicked his knife into the hallway.

Lyla was so confused. The guy who had her attacker held down with a knee to his back looked scarier than the man on the floor. He had on a denim shirt with the sleeves ripped off and greasy hair. He looked like he hadn't showered in a week.

He started barking out orders as if he were in charge. Of what?

Lyla cried out every time the asshole on his stomach made another effort to free himself.

"Handcuffs!" the greasy guy shouted.

The other guy with him handed him a pair.

Rock rushed to Lyla. "Are you okay? Shit, you're bleeding. Keep your hand on the wound, Baby girl."

For a moment, she stared at him wide-eyed.

Rock set a hand on her lower back. "Lyla, Baby, let's get you out of the bathroom."

She grabbed onto him with her free hand. Suddenly, she started gasping. Her body switched out of shocked mode as an emotional burst consumed her.

Rock pulled her into the hallway and hauled her into his arms. "Let me see your neck, Baby girl," he whispered near her ear over the din of shouting.

She eased her hand away.

He winced but pulled off his shirt and pressed it on the wound. "It's okay, Little one. It's not too bad. Look at me."

She was sobbing now, unable to stop herself. Adrenaline pumped through her body, making her shiver violently. Shock.

"Look at me, Lyla," he ordered again.

She forced her gaze to his.

"I've got you. You're safe. The cut isn't bad."

She nodded because he seemed to need her agreement.

Sirens entered her consciousness. Lots of them. They grew louder.

"Who- Who-" She swallowed. "Who are those guys?" She pointed toward the two men who had crowded into the bathroom and now had her attacker cuffed. They were holding him down.

"Police, Baby girl."

She couldn't make sense of that. They didn't look like police.

Rock cupped her face and turned her so she was facing him. "They were undercover. They were following Carl."

"So-so-so that's Carl?"

"Yes."

"Do-do-do you know them?"

"Yes, Little one." He pulled her tighter against him, still holding his shirt to her neck. There wasn't room for them to move. The hallway was jammed with people coming in both directions.

He forced her to continue looking at him. "It's a small town, Lyla. I know most of the people. I've worked with the police several times. I didn't know these guys were tracking Carl until one of them called me about ten minutes ago."

"They called you?" She stared at him, struggling to make sense of all this.

"Yes. They spotted him and were trying to follow him through town. Owen called me to make sure you were safe and with me. When I told him you weren't, I jumped in my car to head here."

"But, if they were undercover, how did they know about me and know to check that I was with you?"

"As soon as Susan realized it was most likely Carl Houseman who had attacked you, she contacted Owen's handler and told him so he could get in touch with Owen and fill him in about our involvement and her suspicions about Carl."

Lyla inhaled deeply. "A lot of people were looking out for us."

"They sure were, Baby girl."

She leaned into Rock hard, letting him absorb her weight. "Jackson…"

As if she conjured him, Jackson suddenly burst through the throng and into the hallway. "Fuck. Jesus. Fuck." He glanced at Rock. "Is she okay?"

"She'll be fine. It's just a nick."

Jackson ran a hand over his head. "Fuck," he growled again. "She just went to the bathroom. I should have gone with her."

Rock grabbed Jackson's arm. "It's not your fault."

Lyla sincerely hoped Rock truly believed that. She didn't want Rock to be furious with Jackson for not going into the damn bathroom with her.

"Police," someone shouted from inside the coffee shop. "Clear out of here, everyone, now. You need to let us get through."

Surprisingly, the hallway cleared, and four officers in uniform came into view.

Rock pulled Lyla back another foot, giving the police room to get through.

Jackson moved with them, closer toward the rear exit next to the men's room.

Lyla tried to stop shaking, but she couldn't. She trembled

violently while everything happened in slow motion around her. Carl was hauled off the floor and escorted out of the bathroom and then out of sight. The police asked a lot of questions, which Rock and Jackson fielded.

A paramedic joined them. "Let me look at your neck, ma'am."

Rock removed his shirt from the wound and tipped her head into the light.

The paramedic took a quick look and then nodded toward the door. "My partner is bringing the ambulance around behind the coffee shop. Let's go out there. I need to see the wound better."

Rock and Jackson flanked her as they led her out of the door and toward the awaiting ambulance.

The paramedic opened the rear door and reached in to drag a first-aid kit to the edge. "Let's have another look, ma'am."

Lyla felt like she was underwater. Everyone's voices were muted.

"I think she's in shock," Rock said. He hopped up onto the back of the open ambulance, sat, and lifted her into his lap. His lips came to her ear. "I've got you. You're safe. Let the medic look at your neck."

The paramedic gently tipped her head to the side.

Lyla winced when something cold touched her.

"Sorry. I'm just cleaning the area. It's a tiny nick. I promise. No need to worry. I'm going to put one butterfly bandage over it. You'll be fine in no time. It won't even scar." The man was very kind, and he took care to keep his motions slow.

Lyla was panting. Her world was spinning.

"There. All done."

Rock guided her head upright. He cupped her face. "You're okay, Baby girl."

She wasn't, though. That was twice Carl had attacked her. She was shaking with fear. Rationally, she knew he'd been taken into custody, but she wasn't feeling rational at the moment.

Jackson handed Rock an open bottle of water, and Rock helped her take several sips. He kissed her temple.

"The police need to speak to her," Jackson said, looking leery. His brows were drawn together as though he didn't think she was capable.

Lyla took in a deep breath and fought for inner strength. She couldn't let Carl get to her like this. He was nobody. An asshole who'd tried to terrorize her. She needed to take back her power.

She nodded. "I'm okay."

"You sure?" Rock asked. "We can wait a while if you need more time."

She shook her head. "No, I'm good."

The two officers who'd come to the house the night Carl attacked her stepped closer.

Susan was the first to speak. "Lyla, I'm so sorry. Are you okay?"

Lyla nodded. "I will be."

"Can you tell us what happened?" Susan asked.

"I went to the bathroom, and as I was coming out, that guy attacked me. He slammed me into the wall and demanded to know where I put his stuff. Just like last time. I don't have any idea what his stuff is." Apparently, the guy was Carl Houseman, but she had no personal way of confirming that. She couldn't remember him well from high school.

"*We* do," Susan said.

Rock held Lyla tighter. "Enlighten us."

"Carl Houseman was in over his head, buying and selling drugs. He got behind. He owed his dealer a lot of money. So, the last time he made an exchange, the guy followed him back to your house. He knew Carl was keeping his stash there, and the house was vacant, so he waited for Carl to leave, went in himself, found the stash, and took everything."

"How the hell did you find all this out?" Jackson asked.

Rock simply nodded. "Because Owen was undercover. He knew, but he couldn't call it in."

Susan nodded. "Exactly."

Lyla turned her gaze toward Rock. "The guy who came in behind you?"

"Yes."

"Is it over, then?" Lyla asked, unable to keep her voice from shaking.

"Yes, Baby girl, it's over."

Susan nodded. "The investigator might have a few more questions for you, but they have most of what they need without you. You can press charges for assault, of course, and that might be advised at some point, but chances are Carl will get nailed for far bigger crimes before anyone could even take a look at your assault charges."

Lyla nodded. "Okay." She certainly didn't want to become involved in a lengthy court battle if it wasn't necessary.

"I'll let you folks get out of here." Susan smiled as she and her partner turned to head back into the coffee shop.

"Let's get you home," Rock stated.

"To your place?" she asked, her voice squeaking.

"To *our* place, Little Lyla." Rock kissed her temple and helped her to her feet.

CHAPTER
TWENTY-TWO

A week later…

"Are you sure about this?" Rock asked Lyla as he sat next to her on the couch.

She was holding her sketchbook. She wasn't just holding it; she had it plastered to her chest with one arm across it as if it contained all her secrets and she was reluctant to let them go. She nodded. "I'm sure."

He angled toward her and stroked a hand down her pony-tail. "Baby girl, you do not have to show me your sketchbook. It's like a diary to you. It's private. I don't want you to feel obligated to show me anything in it."

She shook her head. "It's okay. I want you to see it. I think you'll understand me better if you do. But also, I know what I want my first tattoo to be. It's in here because I sketched it myself. I want you to see it and approve it."

He narrowed his gaze. "You don't need my approval for something like that, Little one." He hated how tense she was, as if she were being forced to do something way out of her comfort zone.

When she lowered the book onto her lap, he pressed a hand over it. "Lyla…"

She lifted her gaze. "It's okay, really. I mean it. It just makes me feel vulnerable, but I don't mind being vulnerable in front of you. You're my man, my partner, my Daddy."

"Okay, Baby girl," he whispered.

"I have dozens of books like this, but this is the latest one I've been using. It was blank when I first arrived here."

He watched her closely, noting the shaking of her hands and the way she smoothed her fingers over the cover of the book as if it were her most precious possession. He had no idea what to expect or why she was so nervous.

It was just a sketchbook. The first time he'd seen her sketching, she'd been working on a fruit basket in her basement. He had no idea what was so private about a fruit basket. What other kinds of things did she sketch?

She opened it to the first page and reverently smoothed her hand over the edge.

Rock's breath hitched as he leaned closer. It was *him*. In her basement. A younger version of him, sitting on the old couch that used to be down there in front of that hideous, blue-carpeted wall. "When did you do this?" he whispered.

"The night I got here. When I arrived at the house, I wandered around for a while. When I went downstairs and saw that carpeting, my knees nearly buckled. I was transported back in time and ended up sitting on the floor sketching for hours. My memories."

"I drove by the house that night. I saw the lights on in the basement, but I figured you'd just forgotten to turn them off when you left." Thank God Carl hadn't attacked her that night. She'd been alone. Who knew what could have happened?

She turned the page. Another sketch of Rock. He was

standing in front of the carpeted wall this time, playing an air guitar.

He chuckled. "That's amazing. How did you pull that out of your mind?"

She shrugged. "I don't know. Even before I came here, I had started thinking about you more. Maybe because I knew I was coming. Maybe it made me feel like I would be close to you. Maybe I hoped I would see you. Maybe I slipped into the past and got trapped. I don't know. The book before this one looks similar, and I wasn't even in town yet. I just follow my muse. I sketch whatever comes to mind."

He was so choked up he could barely breathe. He reached for the book. "May I?"

She released it, letting him hold it in his lap.

He stared at the sketch. He shouldn't have been surprised by her talent. She'd always been talented. He'd seen some of her work. But the likeness to him from nearly forty years ago was uncanny.

After a few pages, he noticed he looked different. Older. These were sketched after they were reunited. When had she had time? Some were of him. Some were of items, like his bike, his jacket, his boots. His cabin in the woods featured in a few. And then he came to several doodles of his MC logo and variations of it. Finally, he noticed a page of teddy bears. Some of them were worn like the one he'd given her years ago. Some were new, like the second one he'd given her the night they'd reunited. One of the older ones was circled.

"What's this, Baby girl?"

"My tattoo."

He lifted his gaze to find her biting her lip.

He cupped her face. "I love it." He looked back down. The bear was worn, but she'd made it somehow look loved and happy. The bear was wearing a T-shirt, and on the T-shirt was his name: Rock.

A lump in his throat kept him from responding. He stared

and stroked the edge of the page, not wanting to mess up her sketch.

"If you don't like it…" she murmured.

He jerked his gaze to hers. "I love it so much, I'm speechless, Little Lyla. Where are you planning to put the tattoo?"

She shrugged. "I did a bit of research. I think it might be too painful on my boob. Maybe here?" She pointed to her bikini line, low on her hip. No one would ever see it but him.

He set the book on the coffee table and grabbed her around the waist to lift her onto his lap, straddling him. Cupping her face, he said, "Marry me."

She smiled. "Okay."

"Yeah?" He sat taller.

"You seem shocked I would agree," she teased, stroking his shoulders.

He shrugged. "You didn't hesitate."

"Why would I? You're the love of my life. I'm not going anywhere."

He pulled her in for a kiss. "When?"

She giggled. "When should we get married?"

"Yes. I was thinking tomorrow."

She giggled harder. "Okay."

He grinned wide. "You'd do that?"

She leaned closer to him. "Yes, Daddy."

He shuddered. He would never get tired of hearing her call him Daddy. He knew it would take time for her to know her Little and settle into a life that included the right balance for them, but she was taking on more and more aspects of age play by the day.

Lyla loved it when he tied her to the chair and fed her. She loved it when he dressed her in naughty lingerie and put adult clothes over it. His favorite was the pink cotton panty and bra set that said Daddy's Baby Girl on the front. He loved that no one but him knew what she was wearing.

She submitted to him deeply when they were home, letting

him bathe her and put sexy Little girl nighties on her. He liked to rock her in the evenings, stroking her hair until she sighed contentedly.

Lyla would probably never be the sort of Little who ran around the clubhouse in a toddler dress with pigtails and ruffled socks, but she was perfect just the way she was, and he adored her.

"Would you rather have a big wedding with your family present?" Jackson had left town several days ago, heading back to New York to wrap up things before he moved to Florida to take over her condo. Nothing could have been tidier.

Rock would take Lyla to Florida as soon as she wanted. They would visit her parents and pick up some of her things, but did she want them at her wedding?

She shook her head. "Nope. I'd rather have something small. Maybe just you and me, Carlee and Atlas, Remi and Kade. We could have a party afterward at the clubhouse?"

"Sounds perfect. When do we tell your parents?"

"We'll call them and Jackson the next day, after it's done." She giggled.

He lifted his brows. "Are you worried they won't approve?"

"No. I'm worried my mother will insist on something elaborate that I'm not in the mood for. I already did that the first time. I just want something intimate with you. Is that okay?" She flattened her hands on his chest.

"It's the best idea I've ever heard. With the exception of the time you agreed to get on my bike and then let me claim your body in my apartment. That was pretty fucking special."

She graced him with a slow, sexy smile. "Maybe we should do that again."

"Which part?"

"Take me for a ride on your bike, and then bring me back here and ravage me."

He grinned, not hesitating to stand with her all wrapped around him.

She slid to the floor. "You can't lift me like that, old man. You'll end up with back problems or some shit."

He chuckled and pulled her into his arms. "As long as I end up with you, I don't care about anything else." He kissed her until they were both panting and moaning.

She finally broke the kiss and leaned back. "Daddy…" she whined, her voice adorable. "First, the bike ride; then, the fucking."

He pinched her butt. "You can't use Daddy and fucking in the same sentence, naughty girl. Unless you want your bottom spanked."

She lifted both brows. "Oh, I definitely want my bottom spanked. Can you do that in between?"

He growled and kissed her again. "I can spank you whenever you want, Little girl."

CHAPTER
TWENTY-THREE

One week later…

"Oh, my heavens. You are so pretty. I love, love, *love* this dress," Ivy said. She was the first to skip toward the door as Lyla entered with Rock—now her husband.

Lyla's face heated as several people rushed toward her. The women were fawning over her. The men were slapping Rock on the back and congratulating him.

Remi and Carlee came in behind Lyla and Rock with their Daddies, Kade and Atlas.

Steele, the club president, took Ivy's hand and kissed it. He was such a softy when it came to his Little. "Let's give them some space, Little girl."

Doc and Gabriel were close by. They had been the first to congratulate Rock.

Talon waved from across the room. "Anyone need a drink?"

The common room had been transformed into the most

beautiful reception space Lyla had ever seen. It helped that everyone in attendance had contributed by chipping in to make this day special with one week's notice.

Brooke had arranged all the pink-and-white flowers that were on the tables. Her Daddy, Storm, was helping her center them.

Eden had ordered the gorgeous pink-and-white tablecloths. Elizabeth had decorated all the chairs with baby's breath and pink flowers.

There was a theme—pink and white. The Littles had been beside themselves with ideas last week when Lyla had told them she wanted soft pastel pink.

There were pink-and-white gifts all over the table. They matched, like a display for a photo shoot. And based on the way Addie was fussing with them, Lyla had to assume she'd wrapped everything and arranged it all to look perfect on the table.

Faust's Little girl, Molly, was standing at the cake table, organizing pink-and-white plates and forks. Faust was next to her, supervising, which cracked Lyla up inside.

Doc's Little girl, Harper, worked at a bakery and had made the cake. Doc and Harper were carrying around plates of cookies.

Sapphire and Ella were the newest Little girls to have met their Daddies, Blade and King. The two of them were wearing aprons and setting the long table for a feast. And Lyla knew it would be an amazing feast because Bear had been in charge of the menu.

Ella handed Lyla a clear plastic cup of punch. It was pink sherbert and lemon-lime soda. King groaned as he carried a tray of pretty punch cups and helped Ella hand them to all the Littles. "So much sugar. I know what happens when you girls get together. The shenanigans go up fifty percent when there's sugar involved."

Lyla giggled and rose onto her tiptoes to kiss King on the

cheek. The punch was delicious. The cake was going to be, too. Even though the outside was white frosting with pretty pink roses, she knew the cake was pink on the inside.

Someone clanked silverware against a glass, and Lyla turned to face that direction with everyone else. It was Atlas. He stepped onto a chair. "I want to say a few words."

The room grew quiet.

Rock wrapped both arms around Lyla from behind, kissed her ear, and whispered, "You're so beautiful, Baby girl. Have I told you that?"

She giggled. He'd told her that about a hundred times.

Atlas cleared his throat. "I just want to say that it's been a long time since I've seen my dad so happy. I'm so grateful for Lyla and whatever spell she cast on him."

Everyone laughed.

Lyla couldn't keep from grinning. Her face hurt from the wide smile she'd worn all day.

"But seriously," Atlas continued, "Lyla, we are so glad to add you to our family and to the Shadowridge Guardians family."

Kade lifted Remi onto a chair next to her brother. He kept his hands on her hips to steady her. Remi lifted her cup of punch. "I couldn't have said it better myself. Lyla, I love you already. You complete our family. Thank you so much for loving my dad and for agreeing to put up with him for the rest of your lives. Also, thanks for taking over the task of making him eat vegetables so I don't have to."

Laughter filled the room again.

Lyla dabbed at her damp eyes with a tissue. She'd had a tissue in her hand for several hours. She'd been through several packs of them. Remi was such a sweetheart. Lyla wouldn't tell her that it would be no hardship convincing Rock to eat healthy. The man was on a quest to be the healthiest human alive, a quest he must have embarked on the moment he was reunited with her.

"Cheers," someone shouted before everyone joined in.

Rock led Lyla to the center of the room and lifted her onto a chair as Atlas and Remi stepped down, putting her above everyone. She flushed, feeling like the center of attention—which she was.

Rock held her hands and looked up at her. "Little Lyla, you may have been gone for many years, but I never forgot you. Thank you for coming home and making me the happiest man on Earth. I will spend every day for the rest of my life doing whatever it takes to make sure you're the happiest Little girl in the world."

Her tears fell in earnest now. She couldn't stop them. When he wrapped his arms around her thighs and lifted her off the chair, holding her high in the air, she grabbed onto his shoulders, looked into his eyes, and said, "I love you, Daddy."

Rock cradled her in his arms and carried her out of the common room, setting her down when they reached the hall-way. He took her hand and guided her to his apartment, where he shut and locked the door.

She giggled. "We can't leave our own party. It's just getting started."

He chuckled as he pulled her into his arms for a kiss. A long kiss. The kind that made her dizzy and horny. When he finally broke it off, he was breathing heavily. "I just needed a few minutes alone with my Baby girl."

"I love you."

"I love you, too, Little Lyla."

"I need you to help me with something before we go back out there."

"What's that, Baby girl?"

She took a step back and pointed down at the full skirt that floated all around her in many layers. She lifted one of the ruffles to expose a button. "See that button?"

He nodded. "Yep."

"There are twelve of them all the way around. Can you unbutton them for me?"

His brow furrowed. "Sure." He squatted down in front of her and began to slide every button through its hole while she slowly turned in a circle. When he was done, the entire bottom half of the dress fell away, leaving her in the cutest Little-girl party dress.

He rose, took a step back, and grinned from ear to ear. "Fuck, that's sexy."

She spun around, letting it fly. Under the dress, she had on a pair of frilly bloomers that matched so that if she bent over too far or twirled too fast, no one would see her panties.

Rock's breath hitched.

She reached up and unfastened the poofy sleeves on both sides, too, changing it into a sleeveless dress that fit right in with what the other Littles were wearing.

Rock licked his lips. "You're full of surprises today."

She held up a finger. "One more thing. Wait here." She flounced into the bathroom, closed the door, and opened the drawer where she'd stashed a few things intentionally for this moment.

It only took her a few minutes to pull back a small section of hair on both sides into little pigtails and add white ribbons. Most of her hair still hung in ringlets down her back, but the front now had a very Little look. She also removed her heels and slipped into the pale-pink ballet flats she'd hidden in another drawer.

When she stepped back into the bedroom, Rock's eyes went wide, and he staggered backward. "Lyla…"

"Do you like it?"

He found his footing and shuffled toward her. "Baby girl, I love everything about you. You're absolutely stunning. Are you sure you're comfortable being dressed like this today?"

She nodded. "I'm totally comfortable and so very happy. It's going to be the best night ever." She was really looking forward to giggling and dancing with all her new friends. She was older than all of them, but no one ever made her feel like she didn't belong. She was grateful to each and every one of them for making her feel like she was part of the family and helping her find her Little.

Lyla didn't imagine she would ever be the sort of Little who rushed around the clubhouse wearing extremely young outfits, but it was fun to occasionally role-play, and tonight was definitely a night to let her Little all the way out.

She grabbed her Daddy's shoulders, rose onto her tiptoes, and kissed him. "I'll be very disappointed if you don't take me aside and spank me at some point tonight," she told him.

He chuckled. "Don't you worry, Little Lyla. I'm certain the other Little girls will talk you into something outrageously naughty before the night is over. Please just promise me you won't climb up in that old oak tree wearing this dress. I'm worried you'll get caught in the ruffles and fall."

"I won't, Daddy. Promise. I think the girls have already plotted something that involves hiding the pretty pink candies and eating way too many of them without permission."

He laughed hard, tipping his head back. "I can live with that. You can use the energy from the sugar high when we get back to the room."

She giggled and kissed all over his face. "That's a promise. We haven't had sex yet today. We still have all four orgasms saved up for tonight."

Rock rubbed his chest. "I'm not sure if my ticker can take that," he joked.

She set her forehead against his and wrapped her arms around him. "It better. I intend to have you chasing me around for several decades."

"I'll do everything in my power to make that happen, Little Lyla. I love you."

"I love you, too, Daddy."

AUTHOR'S NOTE

I hope you've enjoyed the Shadowridge Guardians MC series as much as we enjoyed writing them! Here's a list of all the books in the series in case you missed some!

Shadowridge Guardians MC
Steele by Pepper North
Kade by Kate Oliver
Atlas by Becca Jameson
Doc by Kate Oliver
Gabriel by Becca Jameson
Talon by Pepper North
Bear by Becca Jameson
Faust by Pepper North
Storm by Kate Oliver
Blade by Pepper North
King by Kate Oliver
Rock by Becca Jameson

ALSO BY BECCA JAMESON

The Wilde Heirs:

Ryder

Tiago

Dallas

Brody

Hayes

Blaze

Seattle Doms:

Salacious Exposure by Becca Jameson

Salacious Desires By Kate Oliver

Salacious Attraction by Becca Jameson

Salacious Indulgence by Kate Oliver

Salacious Devotion by Becca Jameson

Salacious Surrender by Kate Oliver

Salacious Dreams by Becca Jameson

Danger Bluff:

Rocco

Hawking

Kestrel

Magnus

Phoenix

Caesar

Roses and Thorns:

Marigold

Oleander

Jasmine

Tulip

Daffodil

Lily

Roses and Thorns Box Set One

Roses and Thorns Box Set Two

Shadowridge Guardians:

Steele by Pepper North

Kade by Kate Oliver

Atlas by Becca Jameson

Doc by Kate Oliver

Gabriel by Becca Jameson

Talon by Pepper North

Bear by Becca Jameson

Faust by Pepper North

Storm by Kate Oliver

Blade by Pepper North

King by Kate Oliver

Rock by Becca Jameson

Blossom Ridge:

Starting Over

Finding Peace

Building Trust

Feeling Brave

Embracing Joy

Accepting Love

Blossom Ridge Box Set One

Blossom Ridge Box Set Two

The Wanderers:

Sanctuary

Refuge

Harbor

Shelter

Hideout

Haven

The Wanderers Box Set One

The Wanderers Box Set Two

Surrender:

Raising Lucy

Teaching Abby

Leaving Roman

Choosing Kellen

Pleasing Josie

Honoring Hudson

Nurturing Britney

Charming Colton

Convincing Leah

Rewarding Avery

Impressing Brett

Guiding Cassandra

Chasing Amber

Controlling Natasha

Provoking Camden

Spoiling Lillian

Surrender Box Set One

Surrender Box Set Two

Surrender Box Set Three

Surrender Box Set Four

Open Skies:

Layover

Redeye

Nonstop

Standby

Takeoff

Jetway

Open Skies Box Set One

Open Skies Box Set Two

Shadow SEALs:

Shadow in the Desert

Shadow in the Darkness

Holt Agency:

Rescued by Becca Jameson

Unchained by KaLyn Cooper

Protected by Becca Jameson

Liberated by KaLyn Cooper

Defended by Becca Jameson

Unrestrained by KaLyn Cooper

Delta Team Three (Special Forces: Operation Alpha):

Destiny's Delta

Canyon Springs:

Caleb's Mate

Hunter's Mate

Mastering Rayne

Trusting Aaron

Claiming London

Sharing Charlotte

Taming Rex

Tempting Elizabeth

Club Zodiac Box Set One

Club Zodiac Box Set Two

Club Zodiac Box Set Three

The Art of Kink:

Pose

Paint

Sculpt

Arcadian Bears:

Grizzly Mountain

Grizzly Beginning

Grizzly Secret

Grizzly Promise

Grizzly Survival

Grizzly Perfection

Arcadian Bears Box Set One

Arcadian Bears Box Set Two

Sleeper SEALs:

Saving Zola

Spring Training:

Catching Zia

Catching Lily

Catching Ava

Spring Training Box Set

The Underground series:

Force

Clinch

Guard

Submit

Thrust

Torque

The Underground Box Set One

The Underground Box Set Two

Wolf Masters series:

Kara's Wolves

Lindsey's Wolves

Jessica's Wolves

Alyssa's Wolves

Tessa's Wolf

Rebecca's Wolves

Melinda's Wolves

Laurie's Wolves

Amanda's Wolves

Sharon's Wolves

Wolf Masters Box Set One

Wolf Masters Box Set Two

Claiming Her series:

The Rules

The Game

The Prize

Claiming Her Box Set

Emergence series:

Bound to be Taken

Bound to be Tamed

Bound to be Tested

Bound to be Tempted

Emergence Box Set

The Fight Club series:

Come

Perv

Need

Hers

Want

Lust

The Fight Club Box Set One

The Fight Club Box Set Two

Wolf Gatherings series:

Tarnished

Dominated

Completed

Redeemed

Abandoned

Betrayed

Wolf Gatherings Box Set One

Wolf Gathering Box Set Two

Durham Wolves series:

Rescue in the Smokies

Fire in the Smokies

Freedom in the Smokies

Durham Wolves Box Set

Stand Alone Books:

Blind with Love

Guarding the Truth

Out of the Smoke

Abducting His Mate

Wolf Trinity

Frostbitten

A Princess for Cale / A Princess for Cain

Severed Dreams

Where Alphas Dominate

ABOUT THE AUTHOR

Becca Jameson is a USA Today best-selling author of over 170 books. She is well-known for her Wolf Masters series, her Fight Club series, and her Surrender series. She currently lives in Houston, Texas, with her husband. Two grown kids pop in every once in a while, too! She is loving this journey and has dabbled in a variety of genres, including paranormal, sports romance, military, reverse harem, dark romance, suspense, dystopian, BDSM, Breeder, and Daddy Dom.

A total night owl, Becca writes late at night, sequestering herself in her office with a glass of red wine and a bar of dark chocolate, her fingers flying across the keyboard as her characters weave their own stories.

During the day--which never starts before ten in the morning!--she can be found walking, running errands, or reading in her favorite hammock chair!

…where Alphas dominate…

Becca's Newsletter Sign-up

Join my Facebook fan group, Becca's Bibliomaniacs, for the most up-to-date information, random excerpts while I work, giveaways, and fun release parties!

Facebook Fan Group:
Becca's Bibliomaniacs

Contact Becca:
www.beccajameson.com
beccajameson4@aol.com

facebook.com/becca.jameson.18
x.com/beccajameson
instagram.com/becca.jameson
bookbub.com/authors/becca-jameson
goodreads.com/beccajameson
amazon.com/author/beccajameson

Printed in Great Britain
by Amazon

59787384R00159